Craving His Love

Black Hills Wolves Book 47

By
Kayleigh Malcolm

Copyright © 2016 by Kayleigh Malcolm
ISBN: 978-1-68361-011-3
Cover art by Fiona Jayde

Published by Decadent Publishing Company, LLC
Look for us online at:
www.decadentpublishing.com

Dedication

For everyone who has risen up from the ashes to start over. You are the brave ones.

Chapter One

J osh Clement stood in the middle of his new store and surveyed the boxes decorating the floor around him. I don't have nearly enough stock to fill this space. His original plan had been to rent a small, quaint space for his shop. When he arrived in town the day before, however, he discovered he was the owner of an abandoned building. Drew Tao, the pack alpha, never mentioned it when Josh originally called to ask permission to move there. Apparently, the building belonged to Josh's family, and, as the only surviving member in town, he inherited the property.

He'd been tempted to ask about his real father but decided against it when Alpha Tao didn't bring it up. Some things were better left alone. This was the start of his new life and he'd made certain his past wouldn't follow him by not leaving any forwarding address. This would be his safe place. Somewhere he'd never have to be afraid to be himself. Somewhere he'd never be found. During his conversation with Drew Tao, he realized the alpha didn't give a damn about Josh's sexuality. Instead, he'd told him to behave himself and not to piss off someone named Gee.

"This is way more space than I need," he muttered as he surveyed the room. Everything in his life had shifted for the better in a matter of a couple of weeks leaving him in constant state of awe. He'd dreamt of one day owning a yarn shop where he could showcase his own knitting designs. Although he had no idea how much business he would actually do in a small town like Los Lobos, he could rely on his online business for the bulk of his sales. There were the sales from knitting patterns he'd designed to help supplement his online income. With an almost nonexistent overhead other than stock, electricity, and water, and the generously sized loft apartment upstairs, he could make this work. It's almost too perfect.

For years, Josh never really lived his life. Instead, he survived it. To suddenly find himself with almost everything he'd ever dreamt of seemed far too good to be true. He'd never really had anything to lose in life, and now all of that had changed. He kept waiting for it to be yanked away from his grasp.

Banishing his gloomy thoughts, he concentrated on moving some of the sturdy wood display tables forward and turning the shelves to create a faux wall across the back of the shop. The small change made the space seem smaller and made his meager stock look less out of place. When Mrs. Arven, the sweet old lady he considered his surrogate grandmother, had to give up her shop and move into a senior's home closer to her children, she left all the remaining inventory to him.

He decided to take a break from unpacking when his stomach grumbled, reminding him he'd skipped lunch. He only had a little bit of snack food in the apartment because in his excitement to get unpacked he hadn't thought of grocery shopping. Letting his wolf free to explore and hunt in the forest around him would solve his hunger, but shifting forms never came easy to him. He needed to be mentally prepared for the stress and anxiety it gave him. *Because I'm used to shifting to avoid getting my ass kicked.*

Locking the shop door gave him a great deal of pleasure. The feel of a key in his hand added to the

3

sense of security he craved. After a quick look up and down the street, he realized his choices were limited. The bakery or diner looked promising but the bar would have beer, something Josh could really go for after a day of cleaning and unpacking.

He glanced up at the name "The Den" hanging over the bar door and remembered Alpha Tao's warning about the owner. That's who I'm not supposed to piss off.

The exact moment Josh stepped into the bar, almost everyone turned and looked at him. The music continued to play as he froze in the doorway, uncertain if he should turn and run. This is what prey feels like. As an Omega, he didn't have a fight-or-flight sense. He always fled. Everyone appeared to go back to their individual conversations but he couldn't shake the itchy feeling across the back of his neck, as if they still watched him. Taking a deep breath, he continued on toward the bar

"What can I get for you?"

Josh looked up...and up at the bartender. A big burly man, obviously with some native ancestry in his blood, stood there with his hand braced on the countertop. Arousal slammed against Josh's senses in a hot rush. Older men turned his crank hard and this guy looked like a walking wet dream.

"You and a twin brother would be a great start."

"There's only one of me, boy."

Please be gay. Please be gay. The deep rumble of the big man's voice coupled with the authoritative tone when he called Josh "boy." Holy crap. If he threatens to spank me, I might just come in my pants.

"One of you is still more than enough for me."

The big guy arched his eyebrow and shook his head. "'Fraid I'm not on the menu."

Disappointment crashed over his senses like a bucket of ice water, deflating his cock faster than a popped balloon. "I'll take a beer, then, please."

"How about you show me some ID first?"

"I'll show you anything you want." The quip shot out of his mouth before he thought to stop it. Freedom from his obsessive former pack and living with humans for so long had loosened his tongue.

"Boy, you're going to get yourself in a heap of trouble with that mouth." He took Josh's driver's license, a frown pulling at his eyebrows as he looked down at it. "Joshua Clement? You Katie Ann Clement's son?"

"You knew my mom?" Horror washed over Josh,

leaving a bitter taste of bile in his throat. Oh God. Please tell me I didn't make a pass at my father. It would be his luck that the first person he met in this town would be the violent man who sired him. Josh didn't have many hard limits when it came to sex, but incest sat at the top of his squick list.

"Yup, she tried to flirt with me when she was about your age, too." He arched his eyebrow as he handed the card back. "Didn't do her any good either."

Relief rolled over him as he took back his ID card. "My mom never told me much about her life here."

The bartender nodded as if Josh confirmed something for him. "Heard she passed away in an accident."

It wasn't a question. Could he be a spy? Why else would he know things about his mom, years after she left this place?

"Yeah, accident, that's what they told me, too." But Josh knew the truth. His mom's death hadn't been an accident. By taking her own life, she'd committed an act so abhorrent to their kind—no one spoke of it. It took years before he came to terms and stopped resenting her for leaving him all alone in the world. An open victim to all the bullies she'd hated.

6

"I'm glad you made it back here." Gee slid a bottle of beer across the counter. "This pack is very different from the one you came from."

"Things have changed a lot here, too, from what I understand."

"Now that's an understatement. I hope you've gotten yourself in to see Drew Tao. Wolves are always welcome here, but it's only proper manners to check in with the alpha first."

"Yes, sir, I did. Spoke to him a week ago about relocating here."

"You the one opening a yarn shop in the old hardware store?"

"Yes, sir."

"Explains why you smell like prey."

Josh almost spewed out a mouthful of beer, swallowing it all down in the last second. "Understandable. I've never thought about it before. I work with a lot of natural fibers, alpaca, wool, angora, nothing wrong with acrylic blends, but I never like the finished product as much as one made from natural fibers."

"Sheep and rabbits? That's some good eats around here, boy. You better be careful before someone decides to take a bite out of you."

"Oh, I wish." The words bypassed his filter and shot out of his mouth. What is wrong with me? Josh's muscles instantly tensed to avoid the strike he knew would be headed his way.

Instead of the violent explosion Josh expected, the big man laughed. "It's safer around here but not that safe. You still need to be careful." He stuck out his hand, "I'm Gee."

Josh swallowed and shook Gee's hand, mentally going over everything he'd said in case anything could be construed as insulting. "It's nice to meet you, Gee." The big man didn't appear to be pissed off, neither had his stepfather right before he flew into one of his famous rages, continuing a conversation with his fists.

"Why do you like to play with prey fibers?"

"I love the feel of them and the smell, although it could explain why I'm always hungry when I'm knitting."

"What can you make?"

"Anything. Shawls, scarves, mitts." Josh pulled out his phone and tapped on the photo gallery, lifting the device so Gee could see some of the pictures. "These are some of the patterns I designed."

Gee took the phone and slid his big finger over the

8

screen, skimming through the images. "Who's this?"

He turned the phone around and Josh saw the picture of him and Mrs. Arven. "She's like my adopted grandmother. I never met my mom's parents."

"Yeah, you did. Trust me, you're better off with the one you chose. Katie Ann's mother was a complete bitch through and through."

Gee might as well have stabbed Josh in the heart. His poor mom had tried to be a good mother but couldn't stand up to the bullies around her any more than Josh could. It explained why she never spoke about her life growing up. "This is going to sound incredibly pathetic, but do you know if I have any family around here? My mom never talked about them."

Gee grunted but didn't say any more. "My daughter has a birthday coming up." He turned the phone to Josh with a picture of one of his lace shawl patterns on it. "It's in a couple months. Can you make this in blue for her?"

"Of course I can." Josh quickly figured out the cost of the materials and how much time he would need to make it. Shit, it wouldn't be cheap because a lot of hours would go into knitting it, and, as a dominant,

Gee would expect it for free.

"You charge me the same as you would anyone else. You need to make a living, too."

Shock stole anything Josh might have said, leaving him feeling insecure and a little unsure navigating the rules in this town. "Well, let me check what I have in stock and how about I get you a quote tomorrow?"

Gee nodded. "Sounds good to me. Her birthday isn't for another four months so there's lots of time."

Someone at the other end of the bar called Gee's name. He gave Josh a quick nod before ambling down. Ambling, strange word for me to think of. But he reminded Josh of a big ole bear ambling through the forest. Shhhiiiiittttt, a bear. Christ, I'm lucky I still have my head.

Living in the isolated pack with his mom, they hadn't welcomed any other species. Josh had only met a couple of different shifters in his lifetime. Like the crazy gorgeous guy in the club bathroom in New York. Josh figured his hookup was a feline of some sort. The way he purred while Josh sucked on his cock was a dead giveaway. Maybe I'll find myself another cat. This time I'd love to feel those vibrations around my cock.

An idea tickled his thoughts—creating a double-knit shawl with a paw theme would be a lot of fun. He pulled a pen from over his ear and started sketching out a graph and a generalized shape of the garment. Designing patterns had a lot more to do with math than anything else. He gained a huge sense of accomplishment taking a bunch of mathematical equations and turning them into something wearable.

A young guy bustled around the bar dropping off plates of food and gathering up the dirty ones. He gave Josh a small smile and, when his scent reached Josh's nose, he returned the smile, his wolf sensing a kindred spirit. As an omega, Josh knew how overwhelming a pack of dominants felt. He watched the young server rushing around taking care of the customers seated at tables. He never spoke, but communicated through the odd nod, facial expressions, and hand signals.

"That's Paul. He can't talk."

Josh turned to the woman leaning against the bar next to him. "What happened to him?" Their kind didn't suffer from diseases or defects. If the guy couldn't talk, then he must have been seriously hurt at some point.

"The old alpha was a sadistic bastard and silenced

him." She waved to Gee. "I'm here to pick up our order."

Josh pushed his beer away, his stomach rolling with nausea. He'd seen enough horror inflicted by dominants in his lifetime, on himself and others. It broke his heart that no matter where he went, the same thing always happened.

"It would never happen now. The new alpha, Drew, is a thousand times better than his sire. I'm Tasha." She held out her hand, turning to face him. A vicious scar mottled her cheek and Josh didn't have to ask who'd injured her.

"Josh Clement. I'm opening the yarn shop down the street."

"I heard about you. Are you going to offer lessons?"

Josh told Tasha about his plans for the shop and she seemed genuinely interested. While they talked, Josh tried not to dwell on Paul's silence or Tasha's scar. Would the Dominants in this pack continue to protect the weaker members or eventually revert to the habits of old? Fear settled over his shoulders. He craved safety and security, but now he wasn't so sure the Black Hills pack could provide it. Maybe his dreams of family and safety were nothing more than naive fantasies?

"Nice to meet you, Josh. See you around." She picked up her order and left.

His appetite vanished as soon as his anxiety spiked. Gee was busy at the end of the bar, so Josh left the money for his beer under his glass and left. Head down, not making eye contact with anyone, he hurried down the street to his shop. Pulling down the blind on the glass door, he locked himself in before running to the back, dodging the multitude of boxes sitting around waiting to be unpacked and sorted onto his shelves.

A stairwell at the back led up to the loft apartment over the store. Josh locked the door at the bottom of the stairs and the one at the top. Feeling a small sliver of security, he pulled all the curtains closed so no one from the street could see into his apartment and then hunched down in a corner of the room. Drew promised him that he wouldn't be hurt here, but seeing both Paul and Tasha unnerved him and the "what ifs" rolled through his mind like fear-inducing thunder.

I wish I'd been born stronger.

Chapter Two

Only the strong survive, Stone. I don't want you to ever fear for your safety.

The sun had set on the sleepy small town of Los Lobos when Stone McKie pulled up in front of Gee's bar. It didn't look much different from his memories. Until two weeks ago, he hadn't set foot in the Black Hills for almost a quarter century. He still remembered packing up his stuff in the middle of the night, his parents' panicked whispers, and being told he couldn't bring all his toys, only whatever he could fit into one small suitcase and his backpack.

As an adult, he understood why his parents had done what they had and the stories he'd heard of Magnum Tao's reign made him thankful to a certain extent. He'd left a part of himself in these hills; they'd been his home, his playground, and his shelter. He had run for days through the trees on four legs and curled up in nests of old roots or rotted out hulls of ancient trees, and moving to Alaska had been a complete shock. It might be a beautiful state in places, but they'd moved north of the tree line where snow or gnarly brush were the only ground cover. As long as Magnum Tao lived, they couldn't come back.

Almost twenty-five years later and Stone had grown up stronger than his parents. He could hold his own in a fight, but he knew he wasn't alpha or enforcer material. The idea of constantly having to fight to hold his position held no interest for him, was nothing his wolf craved. He could be in a room of enforcers and not feel the need to challenge anyone, but he couldn't turn his back on someone who needed his help. Stone had spent most of his life in training. His parents didn't want him to ever be in the position they were, scared and too weak to fight. They were simple people, accountants who were much more cerebral than warrior.

Despite his parents' constant efforts to turn him into a warrior, Stone had the soul of an artist, his chosen medium the canvas of skin. There were a surprising number of good tattoo artists in the north, and he'd learned from as many as he could as he traveled. A couple of years living in Japan allowed him the time to learn some of the millennia old traditional techniques. The thought of carrying on those traditions appealed to him. From a young age, he'd learned life held more value than material stuff. What he truly needed, he could fit into the cab of his truck. Memories and dreams were locked in his heart, untouchable by thieves or vandals.

The scents in Gee's bar brought back memories, not all of them good. A vivid memory of being pushed behind his father as a larger man snarled and snapped at him rushed through his mind. Pushing those thoughts away, he took in the ambiance. The same mounted animals adorned the walls, although there might have been a few new trophies. He couldn't remember why his dad would bring him into a bar, but it could have been something as simple as picking up paperwork at tax time.

The bar seemed smaller than he remembered and the distinct aroma of lemon, tea, and prey colored the room. That's strange. He would have thought any prey shifter with a lick of self-preservation would have been terrified to step into a room filled with predators.

A hulking man stood behind the bar, looking as if he'd stepped straight out of Stone's memories. "Gee?

Other than a couple of gray hairs, you old bear, you look exactly the same."

The big man laughed and came around the bar, giving Stone a quick hug and slap on the back, almost knocking the wind out of him. "Look at you, Stone McKie. All grown up and back home. You're a younger version of father."

"I missed the hills." Stone had spent the last couple of weeks in wolf form, exploring his old haunts and reacquainting himself with the Black Hills.

"Many homesick wolves are making their way back. Have you spoken to our new alpha yet?"

The way he said it made Stone wonder if some were coming back not knowing Magnus was dead. "When I first got here, he let me leave my truck behind the barn. I wanted to check everything out before I decided to make it permanent."

"Where are you planning on staying?"

Stone glanced up at the railing above the bar. A stairwell along the one wall led to the second-floor rooms over the kitchens. As a kid, the setup had reminded Stone of a saloon in the Old West. Only he'd been too young to understand why an Old West bar would have bedrooms available.

17

"I hoped you still rented out space upstairs."

"Sure, I'll add it to your tab. You can pay when you check out." Gee left for a moment and then came with a ring holding two keys. "There's an outside stairwell if you want access when the bar is closed, the other key is for the last door at the end of the hall. It's yours for as long as you're here."

"Thanks." Stone tucked the keys into his pocket as Gee poured him a frosty beer. He took a quick look around. A couple of pool tables in the back were occupied as well as most of the dining tables. It appeared Gee did a brisk business; there were more people around than he'd expected.

"What are your plans now you're home?"

Home. The word resonated with Stone on a soul-deep level. He loved these hills and tearing around them the last couple weeks reminded him why. Gee placed the beer in front of him and Stone nodded his thanks. "Thinking of opening my own studio, I'm going to ask Drew if I can rent out the building down the street, the one with the apartment above it."

"You're a couple days too late. One of the Clements found his way back and claimed it."

"Shit. I'll have to talk to Drew and see what else is available." He took a deep breath and huffed in frustration. There's the scent again...rabbit and lamb. It made him hungry.

"Is the kitchen still open, Gee?"

The big man nodded, waved at a young guy and then pointed at Stone. He'd already heard about the Den's limited bar menu, deep-fried pickles and a burger. Sounded delicious and exactly what he needed. He caught the server's eye and held up two fingers. Hunting his share of rabbits over the past week kept him from starving, but he wanted more. He couldn't shake the almost-sensual hunger burning in his chest every time he caught the unique prey scent. His wolf paced around restlessly in his head in anticipation of something. This is weird.

He fingered the edge of a napkin left on the bar, focusing on the design. Someone had written a bunch of numbers, symbols, and a sketch of what looked like a 16-bit bear paw. He understood the need to get ideas down on paper when inspiration struck. He carried a small notebook in his truck for when an idea for a tattoo design struck him, usually at red lights or after a long drive.

Gee ambled down the bar and Stone caught his eye. "So Drew Tao keeps a tight rein on his people, huh?"

The old man's eyebrow twitched. "What makes you think that?"

"I've never scented prey in a Pack bar before. They must be confident no one is going to get out of hand and put them on the menu."

Gee grumbled and snorted, which sounded suspiciously like a sarcastic laugh. "Older but not smarter."

He left Stone to staring at his back as he ambled down to get a beer for someone else. What the hell did that mean? He rethought his question and didn't see what part would be funny. Gee didn't come back to clarify his statement, leaving Stone sitting at the bar with an ice-cold beer and the delectable aroma of lamb tempting him. He glanced around, wondering who carried the unique scent, but didn't see anyone who looked like a prey animal. They all tended to have a certain look to them, and Stone would have sworn the bar was filled with wolves.

At a closer look, there were a couple humans milling about with mating bites on their neck, which explained their presence. Stone didn't live like a monk, far from it, but until this moment, no one ever piqued his wolf's interest. Which didn't explain why his wolf's hackles were up. His inner animal rubbed against his human senses, warning Stone he'd missed something vitally important.

The clatter of cutlery sliding on a plate caught his attention, as the young server set a plate with an incredible-smelling burger in front of him. A quick inhale let him know neither it nor the server was the source of the delectable prey scent. Gee didn't offer much on his menu, but what he served always tasted delicious. A quick peek under the bun and Stone did a mental fist pump. Cheese day. He vaguely remembered cheese appeared on burgers sporadically around here. Even with the incredible scent of medium-rare beef and cheese wafting in front of him, Stone still couldn't get the scent of rabbit and lamb out of his nose. "I've spent too much time as a wolf lately," he muttered to himself. The only rational excuse why he couldn't get the intoxicating scent out of his brain.

A very different and strongly dominant scent surrounded him moments before his alpha stepped up and sat down on the stool next to him.

"Hey, Stone, nice to see you on two legs for a change." Drew nodded at Gee.

Stone lifted his burger, letting Drew know a mouth full of food delayed his response. His alpha chuckled.

"Cheese day, huh? I don't blame you. A bit of grilled cow will do you good. I heard you've pretty much been wolf since we spoke?"

Stone chewed carefully and swallowed before speaking. "I wanted to explore the Hills and be sure coming back would be the right decision."

"You mean you wanted to sneak around and see for yourself if I'm full of shit and people were covering for me? It's okay. I understand. You're not the first person to come back wondering if I truly am my father's son."

Stone shrugged. Drew hit the truth right away. "I'm curious about the prey animals you let come around? How are you keeping them safe?"

"Prey shifters?" Drew glanced over at Gee who gave him a look Stone couldn't decipher.

Drew slapped him on the back, the impact vibrating through Stone's chest. The intense alpha energy resonated with both him and his wolf. "Good. I'm looking for some more pack protectors. Interested?"

Wow, that's a big commitment. Stone didn't plan to leave the Hills any time soon. Something about the area calmed his wolf. Maybe this is exactly where I'm supposed to be. He noticed Drew hadn't answered his question regarding the prey shifters who'd moved into the area. Perhaps his offer to make him a pack protector was the enigmatic alpha's way of answering.

"I'd like that." It would also give him a place in the pack and allow him to build on his tattoo business. "Gee said the empty store down the street has been taken."

Drew nodded. "Josh Clement spoke to me a couple of weeks ago. It used to be owned by his grandparents so I thought it would give him a sense of family."

"Not likely," Gee snorted before lumbering away. Stone didn't understand the cryptic comment, but he remembered his dad's comments about Gee. *He knows more about this town and the people in it than he'll ever let on.*

"There's a lot of square footage in his building and I'm not sure how much space Josh needs. You could ask him. Maybe he'll be interested in renting out some space."

"That's not a bad idea." Stone had contemplated doing the same thing when he'd originally looked at the empty building. "What business is he running anyways?"

Drew shrugged one shoulder and jerked his head. "Something to do with a lot of string and craft stuff."

It wouldn't be the first time Stone rented out space in an established business. In all honestly, he didn't need much room for himself. Really, how much room could this guy need if his stock consists of string? It sounded like a pretty bizarre business venture, and Stone figured Josh was probably old and looking more for something to keep him busy rather than building an actual business. "Thanks for the idea. I'll speak to him. If all he's selling is string, he might be interested in bringing in some additional income."

"Good. Stop by the barn tomorrow and we'll talk more about your place in the pack."

Drew moved off to speak with a few other people who were waiting for him, giving Stone a chance to finish off his burger. The menu might be limited here but thankfully what Gee did serve tasted amazing. Tossing a few bills on the counter he lifted his hand to the big man in thanks. Gee nodded in acknowledgement before returning to his business.

Stone made a couple trips to his truck, bringing a few bags up to his room. He kept the majority of his equipment locked safely in his truck with the alarm set. Clothes he could replace, his tattoo guns were

24

part of him. If he lost those it would be like trying to create art without any medium.

The bar noise echoed up the stairs but, when he closed the door to his room, the sound diminished greatly. That's some damn good insulation. A simple double bed sat against one wall across from a long window that, upon closer inspection, looked out over the main street. A few lights were on in the building he'd wanted to rent. Paper covered the windows, preventing him from seeing inside, but a shadow slid across it every once in a while.

He glanced at the digital clock on the nightstand. Eight thirty, not too late to say hello to the owner and let the guy know about his interest in renting out part of his building. Stone didn't see the point in waiting to do something tomorrow when he could get a head start on it right now. This way he could spend tomorrow making alternative plans if this tactic didn't pan out. It only took a minute to dump the contents of his bags into the set of drawers before sliding the empty duffle bags under the bed.

The fresh, crisp air heralded the distinct chill of winter; thousands of stars dusted the night sky encouraging Stone to stop and admire them. How do people live in cities and miss out on the natural beauty above them? In Alaska, he'd spent hours staring up at the sky trying to count the starts or sketch the northern lights. A simple drawing couldn't capture the real elements. They needed to be experienced to be appreciated.

His mouth watered as he approached the shop front. The distinct scent of prey coated the air here. I wonder if this is why Drew encouraged me to ask Josh about renting. Maybe he wanted a pack protector close by to take care of the little lamb or rabbit.

A small shadow moved across the paper-covered window, and he could hear someone inside humming an unrecognizable tune. His future landlord couldn't hum on key, decimating the song running through his head.

Mine.

Stone stumbled at his wolf's strong announcement. Up until now, the delicate aroma had kept his primal side content. But, now, a ravenous hunger emanated from that part of his psyche. We are not going to eat our potential landlord. A sharp rap on the door and everything inside stilled. He knocked again and this time called out, "Josh Clement? My name is Stone McKie. Drew Tao sent me over. Can I speak to you for a moment?"

A slight shuffle ruffled the paper on the door, and he heard the telltale sound of a lock being turned. The door opened revealing, not the crazy old man Stone expected. Instead a vision of innocence and perfection filled the doorway. The young man only came up to his shoulders, with high cheekbones, full lips, and the longest black lashes Stone had ever seen on a male. Josh Clement looked almost too delicate to be a man. Hundreds of thin dreadlocks in shades of brown and dark blond were tied back from his face by a wide, colorful bandana. But, his scent made Stone's blood roar in his ears and his cock thicken. A delicious prey scent intermixed with the headier aroma of wolf. The complex combination enthralled him.

Mine.

Stone knew what his wolf tried to say and welcomed the idea of getting naked and nasty with the man in front of him. He stepped forward and Josh stepped back. Unease wavered along the edges of his scent, but a decadent heady arousal encouraged Stone to get closer. He has to be feeling this, too. Closing the distance between them, he wrapped his hand around the back of Josh's neck under his dreadlocks, preventing him from retreating.

"You said Drew sent you. Who are you?" The words were almost a whisper. Stone didn't want to speak. He focused on his mate's plush lips while images of pressing his cock between them filled his head.

"I'm all yours, bunny." The endearment seemed appropriate since the rabbit scent still clung to the smaller man like cologne. "And you're all mine."

The moment their lips touched, Stone lost all control. His wolf surged to the surface of his consciousness and Stone fought to keep him in check. It felt like every single instance of joy in his life surged into this one moment, the ultimate gift from fate. He wanted to touch his mate, rub his scent all over him. He buried his nose against the sensitive skin behind his mate's ear. "God, you smell so good, I could take a bite out of you."

Sliding his hands down his slim mate's body, he cupped his round ass and lifted him up, mashing their groins together, grinding them together as he claimed kiss after kiss. Josh let out a small whimper, and Stone vaguely noticed the frantic movements against him. His mate was obviously as excited and he couldn't wait to feel his hands on his chest and closing around his cock. "You're all mine and I'm going to fuck you in every room until neither of us has the ability to walk. Then we can get to know each other more."

He let Josh slide down his body until his feet touched the ground. "Where is the closest bed?" He planned to claim Josh in every room, but their first time would be in a bed. He would love and protect his mate, but he wouldn't sully their first time by fucking him hard against the nearest wall like a bar toy.

"No, wait."

The words echoed in Stone's head but didn't sink in. His wolf still pressed to claim his mate and didn't understand any need to delay things. "Don't worry. I'll get cock deep in you soon enough. A few seconds to make it to your room won't change anything."

His wolf rode him hard as his blood rushed through his body and his cock throbbed with a pulse all its own. With his hand holding Josh's arm, he looked around for the way leading upstairs. A single breath later, Josh twisted, and a heavy, blunt weight drove up between Stone's legs. Between heartbeats, the most excruciating pain radiated from his balls, stealing his breath and sent him retching to the floor.

***

A flash of guilt-ridden sympathy twisted in Josh's chest when Stone dropped to his knees cupping his crotch, harsh gagging noise the only sound he made. He'd panicked when the huge man rushed him, the memory of the omegas from the bar and what had been done to them, so fresh in his mind. When Stone's features went primal, Josh's wolf cowered in the back of his mind at what it perceived as an attack by a dominant.

Fear slammed through Josh like an icy spike. What have I done? Josh could endure his stepfather's beatings, but he wouldn't survive Stone's strength. By kneeing the large man in the nuts, he'd signed his own death certificate. Better to get out of there as fast as possible. His wolf scrambled against his consciousness, begging him to get moving, to run.

"You little fuck. I'm going to kick your ass." The words were more of a groan than spoken. The larger man's amber eyes went completely wolf, fury radiating from his scent and expression.

Run! Josh's sense of self-preservation ripped through the terror-fueled paralysis, forcing his limbs into action. Tearing down the street, he stumbled

30

when his name echoed in the night air. The angry snarl behind him encouraged his muscles to work harder, his very life depending on his ability to escape. Josh didn't turn around, didn't want to know how quickly the distance closed between them. Running had never done him any good in the past, but it never stopped him from trying. He needed more speed and could only get that on four legs.

Angling away from the buildings he headed straight for the tree line. Tearing off his shirt, he shifted into his furry self. His thinner hind legs left his pants and shoes behind as he darted for the trees. His only hope right now was to hide until the worst of Stone's fury abated. He'd learned the trick from dealing with his stepfather, Donnovan. A beating later on would never be as bad as the beating you get in the heat of the moment. A lesson he'd believed his mother never learned, until he got older and realized she'd used herself to run interference for him.

With every step, one thought echoed wildly in his head. I have nowhere to go. Donnovan and the other enforcers wouldn't dare set foot in Los Lobos without talking to Drew first. His dreams of a safe home were shattered. When Josh spoke to Drew Tao about moving here, he'd gotten the impression the omegas were treated better than they were in his old home. After seeing Paul and Tasha earlier and then experiencing Stone's forceful behaviour.... I've jumped from the frying pan into the fire.

When he managed to put some distance between him and the dominant male, he started circling back on his trail, in hope of confusing the angry wolf. Most of the enforcers in his old pack were big on muscles and small on brains, and he prayed Stone suffered the same lack of intelligence. He'd never meant to lead Stone on, but the intensity of the moment overwhelmed him.

He'd opened the door and discovered every fantasy-induced wet dream standing on his doorstep. Broad shoulders, tattoos peeking out from under shirtsleeves, a soft, neatly trimmed beard framing a set of plush lips that looked to have been made specifically for soft, playful kisses. The big man radiated a raw sexuality, which perked his interest and woke up a dormant libido. But, it hadn't taken long for the asshole to show his true colors. Attacking and demanding without a single hello. He went from being a living breathing fantasy to his worst nightmare between heartbeats.

His lupine heritage came in handy when he

needed to protect himself against humans while living on the streets. Trying to fight against a large, incredibly dominant wolf, he wouldn't have stood a chance.

Panting, he slowed his pace and started looking for somewhere he could hide. He didn't have the luxury of panicking right now. Creeping between the trees he concentrated on moving silently, listening to the normal woodland sounds around him. Those were all dangerously quiet, as if all the animals knew a predator hunted the forest and they didn't want to get caught in the crossfire. The odd cricket sounded a warning as he moved, but anything considered prey hunkered down and hid. Which is exactly what I should be doing.

A partially rotted fallen tree offered the best coverage. The underbrush had started to reclaim it and backing up into the shadows allowed Josh the chance to watch everywhere out front. With the tree at his back, he didn't have to worry about a rear attack. Prone on his belly, he could hear his heartbeat racing; his wolf wasn't about to let down its guard yet. Despite the exhaustion causing his limbs to shake, he pressed his paws against the cool earth, preparing to run at any moment. His fur insulated him against the cold but not against the icy fear pumping through his veins.

If he'd been human, he would have been one of those pale kids in and out of the hospital, never more than a few inches away from an inhaler. Instead, he'd been born into a species who valued strength and dominance. His mother ran from these hills because Josh's father had changed into a twisted, evil man, devoted to no one but his alpha. Making the same mistake as thousands of women, she thought getting pregnant would change her lover. She'd never told him the truth of what happened to make her leave or even told Josh his father's name because she didn't want him to be tempted to go look for him. *But I did, and look where I am now.*

Ironically, she fell into another pack just as dangerous. After his mom died in the car accident, Josh really learned what kind of man she'd married and the lengths she'd gone to to protect him from knowing the truth. Donnovan Talonski was a violent drunk who hated anything he perceived as weakness.

After her death, Donnovan proved how much Josh disgusted him. While his mother had been afraid to leave, Josh refused to allow himself to be continually beaten. Less than a week after her death, Donnovan brought in a doctor for what they called deprogramming. As if Josh had chosen to be gay to spite the narrow-minded asshole. Two bouts of psychotherapy, one shock treatment, and one brutal beating; Josh left but not without a final fuck you to the old man.

If only I had just left.

But, no. He'd wanted to do something to fuck over the nasty bastard. A small token of retribution, in the name of his mother, he realized now was a stupid mistake. If he could redo it, he would have left and never broken into Donnovan's safe. Then he would never have needed to come to Los Lobos and wouldn't be out in the cold night, hiding under a rotting log and praying for his life.

The minutes passed and Josh started to relax. He might have lost Stone and granted himself a bit of a reprieve. Odds were Stone would trash his store in retribution, but he wouldn't find the money Josh hid or the large ring he'd stolen from Donnovan. Those were hidden under a loose floorboard in his bedroom. I can sneak into town, grab my savings, and take off. Leave everything he'd built and created, disappearing once again. This time he would make sure he went somewhere no one knew him and changed his name.

A low growl was his only warning before an immense black and gray wolf stuck his muzzle under the log and sniffed. Josh didn't wait to see his eyes. He shot out the other side, cursing himself for getting lost in thought and not listening carefully enough to his surroundings. Stone crashed through the underbrush behind him and Josh concentrated on putting his feet in front of each other, darting around trees, pushing his body to the point of collapse as he raced under fallen logs and leapt over brambles. The large male never gave up, never stopped, remaining a short distance behind Josh. Until Stone decided chasing him to be too much effort, Josh couldn't stop. The moment he did, his beating would start.

***

Stone followed his little mate, confused and angry at the terror tainting the air around him. Getting kneed in the balls in the middle of the most life-changing moment of his life had been more than a little jarring. Once the nausea passed and he took a deep breath, he almost gagged at the putrid scent of terror.

What the hell scared Josh so much? Stone could

admit he came on a bit aggressive. Being so close to his mate proved a bigger temptation than he could resist. After decades of searching without any luck, he'd gotten used to having boy toys hanging around the shop, some becoming apprentices then moving on. Others simply continued on with their lives once they realized the life of a tattoo artist wasn't as exciting as the reality TV shows made it out to be. A lot of flash work and belly-button piercings kept a roof over their head. Expensive custom pieces weren't as common as everyone believed.

But fate gave him an artist for a mate. They didn't share the same medium, but Josh would understand when his creative side demanded he pay it proper attention. The napkin he found on the bar must have been Josh's work. That would explain why he couldn't shake his obsession with the delicious scent there. Stone didn't have a clue what the little markings meant, but it must have been Josh planning something his muse demanded.

There'd been a connection. The moment the little twink wiggled his ass under his hand, he'd known it. He also knew he owed Josh an apology for practically attacking him moments after the door opened, but Josh's acute terror confused him.

Fate wouldn't give me a homophobic mate...would they?

They most certainly would. One thing Stone learned in life is fate liked to fuck with him. While chasing his mate through the woods, he replayed every moment he could remember. At first Josh had responded to his touch, sinking against him. He'd never forget the heady scent of arousal in the air, but when his wolf pushed forward, things went wrong. Stone led his wolf take the lead and Josh took off. Stone knew deep down if he let Josh hide now, it would take an extra-long time to get his pup back. He'd already managed to damage something delicate between them and wanted to fix it right away.

It took a good hour to pick up his mate's scent. Josh's talents extended to muddling his trail and covering his tracks, but Stone had learned to hunt across frozen tundra. He knew how to look for more clues than his nose gave him. In his arrogance, he made a second vital mistake by shoving his nose under a fallen log when he picked up the trail. His gentle mate took off like a bat out of hell. The chase continued for another three hours, and he kept a constant space between them. It wouldn't have been difficult to overtake Josh in the first couple of minutes, but he didn't want to throw his strength around and frighten his mate any more. The longer Josh ran, the more apparent he didn't have any plans to stop. When Stone noticed Josh's legs start to shake slightly as they moved, he knew this chase needed to end before Josh tripped and killed himself.

With an easy burst of power, he leapt forward and tackled the exhausted wolf, taking him easily to the ground, careful not to crush the smaller wolf under his body. Josh lay there, curled up in a small ball shaking, his muzzle buried under his paws as he whimpered in terror. His entire body quivered, sending a white-hot rush of anger slamming through Stone's system. His earlier anger melted away as the truth dawned on him. Someone had abused his mate. The idea of anyone lifting a fist to his boy made him want to demand who did it and then tear them a new one.

Josh must have scented his anger because he whined and curled up tighter. Stone shifted into his human form, figuring smaller teeth might appear less aggressive. He wanted to comfort his mate and not terrify him any further.

"SSShhhhh, Josh." He ran his hand over Josh's head and down his spine, feeling bone-deep shivers racking the small wolf's body. "What has you so scared, little one? What did I do?"

Josh lifted his muzzle a touch, enough for one eye to peek out from under his paw. The simple look spoke volumes and, for a moment, a bit of humor glinted off the edges of his thoughts.

"Yes, I did come on a little strong."

Josh peered out over his leg before disappearing under his paw again.

"Okay, perhaps a little over the top. Josh, you're my mate and I couldn't believe my luck. I'm sorry if I scared you when I threatened you. It was an automatic response to having my balls shoved into my throat." He scratched the wolf between the ears. "But I would never hurt you. Ever. You're mine. My mate. I'd protect you with every breath in my body." Taking a chance, he scooped the bundle of quivering fur into his arms and laid his cheek against the top of the slim wolf's head. "Calm down. You've run yourself to exhaustion. Let your wolf protect you, too, and when you're ready you can shift and come to me. We can talk and sort this out."

That might have helped a bit because Josh lifted his face a bit more, exposing his muzzle. Those warm eyes watched him, wary of any movement. If Stone understood the look, his mate didn't believe him at all.

"I swear I won't hurt you." The night settled in and the air grew colder as fall's crisp warning of winter settled around them. "It's late and I think you're going to be too tired to make it back to town, so I vote we curl up here, together. We'll stay warmer and then, tomorrow, I want to have a nice long talk. We have a lot to sort out."

Josh didn't blink his eyes or change his expression. Stone didn't want to be insulted or pissed off, but his mate had convicted him of some crime in his head without talking to him. "If you'd told me to stop, then I would have listened." His balls were still aching from his mate's narrow knee. He ran his hand over Josh's muzzle and his head and lean body. His tawny fur was a beautiful combination of different shades. The fine quivering continued through Josh's muscles, as if his mate prepared to bolt again. He'd been in the middle of the most intoxicating kiss of his entire life when it had fallen completely apart.

He remembered his wolf yanking at his self-control, wanting to wrestle with his gorgeous mate. Stone knew his wolf would physically manifest over his features at times. The moon didn't hold any control over him, and his wolf liked to push his boundaries sometimes. Why would Josh be frightened by my wolf?

Unless someone abused my mate, creating a deep fear in his subconscious. I'm going to kill the bastard if I ever find him. But it wouldn't fix his current problem. He terrified his mate. His inner wolf shuffled and whimpered at the perceived rejection. Trust, he needed to earn his mate's trust before they went any further. Holding himself back wouldn't be easy. He'd spent his life demanding excellence from himself by charging forward. Now, he needed to wait until his mate trusted him.

Spearing his fingers through Josh's fur and curving them over his large head, he gently scratched behind his ears. No one can resist this. Hell, Stone would do anything for a good belly scratch at times. The wolf under his hand stretched and arched his neck, a subtle showing of submission to a dominant wolf.

"You're not going to make this easy on me are you, sweetheart?"

The wind whipped through the forest, raising goose bumps on his arms. He wouldn't die of exposure, but Stone much preferred the warmth of his fur to the chill in the air. "I know you're nervous, baby. I don't want to stay in my skin much longer. I need you to trust me. I'll never do anything to you until you're ready."

He shifted back into his animal form, the layers of fat and fur insulating him better than any ski jacket. The leaves were a nice nest and he curled up behind his mate, stretching his body around Josh's both as a way to share and to conserve heat between them. Josh's wolf stiffened up and lay perfectly still. When it became obvious Stone had no intention of making sexual advances, Josh relaxed slightly. His breathing evened out as his body sank into the sleep he so desperately needed. It took much longer for Stone. Even in wolf form, he had a hard time maintaining control over his cock. With his body wrapped around Josh, a distinct bolt of self-preservation washed over Stone. This traumatized wolf was his mate. His partner. He'd do anything for him, including protecting him from anyone who might cause him the slightest stress. The temperature dropped around them. Stone kept his mate safe and warm. Dawn splintered the black of night as he finally drifted off.

Before he opened his eyes in the morning, Stone knew his timid mate had snuck away at some point in the last few hours. The leaves next to him were flattened from his body, but his warmth had dissipated from the ground. The faint remaining hints of Josh's scent tantalized Stone's senses. As much as he hated drinking alone, he hated sleeping alone even more.

I need to find that little shit and teach him some manners. Preferably naked with him over my knee, the sweet ass of his bared for the world to see and pink from my hand.

Stone's wolf snarled and snapped at his thoughts. No one else would ever see his sweet mate's ass and the sooner he could bite the brave young male, the better. But, those kinds of games would have to wait. We have some serious trust issues to work out.

Stone knew where he could find his gentle mate. And Josh was his mate, no misgivings, or questions about that. Spending the last few hours together curled up in wolf form had made it abundantly clear. Even now, waking up, his animal side scrambled for control, demanding he follow the sweet omega and mark him before someone else got to him. Josh's fear colored his every action. He needed a keeper, or better yet a protector, and Stone could be exactly what his mate needed.

Stone had spent the last month scouring these hills and reacquainting himself with the entire area but, until last night, it hadn't truly felt like home. Meeting Josh changed every aspect of his life. His nomadic days were done, so were the days of hiding up in the barren Alaska landscape. Josh, Los Lobos, and the Black Hills were his home now. Fate gave him a gentle wolf that smelled like prey and had been abused. Josh's mannerisms and the way he ran when Stone started to lose control screamed the truth. Knowing his mate feared him upset him and his wolf the most.

He stood and stretched his back, brushing leaves out of his hair. His years exploring the frozen Alaskan tundra taught him the value in the ability to shift and manifest clothing at the same time. Like humans, there were many different kinds of shifters with a cornucopia of abilities. He'd learned how to keep his clothes with him when he shifted because no one wanted to be bare assed north of the Arctic Circle. That kind of shrinkage was terrible for the ego.

As he trudged through the forest, his thoughts circled around the most important thing in his life at the moment. What to do about Josh. He knew Josh would try to avoid him. Courting and dating were useless gestures in their world. When you met the other half of your soul, you didn't knee him in the balls and take off running for the hills. But apparently Josh didn't get that memo. Now, he needed to figure out a way to convince Josh he didn't have a dominant monster for a mate.

The path he took angled down toward the edge of the river. A soft mewling noise cut through his thoughts and he looked around wondering how the hell a kitten made it into a forest all alone. Following the sounds, which grew weaker every moment, he discovered the corner of a tattered garbage bag sticking out from under a fallen log, the plastic shredded from wild creatures in search of a meal. His nose picked up the scent of several creatures and the remnants of their prey, but it appeared they'd missed one.

He pulled back layers of plastic and revealed a tiny white kitten. Dangerously cold, its heartbeat so faint he thought it was dead until he lifted it up to his ear to listen. The small gasps for air told him there might not be much chance for survival, but he couldn't leave it here to die. *The piece of shit behind this better pray we don't cross paths.* He couldn't detect any scents lingering in the air around him, so they must have tossed the bag to the shore from a boat or canoe.

He tucked the tiny creature into his shirt pocket, hoping the heat from his body would help to warm it. It also reminded him of a cartoon from when he was a kid. "George." He rested his hand over the small bump in his pocket. "I'm going to name you George and I will hug you and pet you and squeeze you."

He left the forest two hours later; they'd covered miles during the pursuit last night. By then, Stone really started to worry about his buddy. George's tiny body had warmed up a bit, but the little guy hadn't moved for the last twenty minutes. Stone didn't want to take him out of his pocket over and over to check his heart rate, despite the incredible temptation. There was another bright shining reason he wanted the tiny bundle of fur to survive. Josh owned a string shop...what better than to have a kitten around and then perhaps his gentle mate wouldn't see him as a monster. He headed directly to the building Josh hid in. The closer he got, the more pungent the smell of prey became. It would have disguised his mate, but burying his face in Josh's tawny fur last night embedded his unique scent to memory.

***

47

A small chime rang when Stone entered. The unlocked door surprised and then annoyed him. What would stop anyone from coming in and hurting Josh? Stone focused on getting his mate's attention, meaning he would have to use some creative tactics. Finding George had been a stroke of luck he hoped would be strong enough to keep Josh from running away.

"Josh, where are you?" He stood in the middle of the store and listened. A faint creak echoed in the ceiling above him and Stone looked up. "There is no reason for you to hide from me. You should have locked the front door because I'm not leaving until you come down and talk. I need your help."

"Shit."

He heard the faint curse then more movement upstairs. The sound of locks turning near the back of the room caught his attention, and, when Stone investigated, he realized the door he assumed was a closet led to a stairwell. More locks clicked before the door opened. If Stone hadn't already figured out his mate had been abused, the number of locks clicking open would have alerted him. Anger at the bastards who abused his mate rushed to the surface, forcing him too quickly to slam down his instincts before frightening Josh again.

"What can I help you with?" Josh stepped through the doorway. His dreadlocks were tied back with another wide colorful scarf. His T-shirt molded to his lean chest, the waistband of his cargo pants sat on his hips, exposing a thin strip of skin. Again, Stone's wolf lunged to the front of his thoughts, focused on the strip of tantalizing skin. Better prepared this time, he wrenched control back. I will not overwhelm him. Not an easy feat when all the blood in his head rushed to his cock as he contemplated how easy it would be to tug those pants down and discover if Josh went commando.

"Stone, you said you needed help?"

"This little guy." Stone lifted the small body out of his shirt pocket, instantly catching Josh's attention. "I found him down by the river all by himself."

The tiny creature let out a miniscule mew and it might as well have been a magnetic force, because Josh moved in front of him a second later. The subtle note of lanolin and chamomile flooded Stone's nose, calming his wolf for the first time all day.

"Poor baby." Josh held up his hands and Stone deposited the kitten against his palms. He brought the kitten up to his neck, and the little thing started purring and rubbing its face against his skin. "Did you see the mother around?"

"No." Stone didn't bother to mention the torn up plastic bag he'd found the kitten in or the remains of his siblings. "There weren't any other scents to prove she'd been there."

"He's practically a newborn; his eyes aren't even open yet. You need to get kitten formula and some bottles."

"Really? Can't we just give him some milk and cat food?" Stone didn't know a damn thing about domesticated animals.

"Cat food?" Josh looked at him as if he'd lost his mind, avoiding direct eye contact for more than a second. "He's a baby. It will be a few weeks before he can handle anything that solid, and I'm not sure cow's milk is really the best thing for him."

"I grew up around predators," Stone blurted out, internally cringing, but unable to stop babbling." In Alaska, the jackrabbits are bigger than most dogs. I have no idea what to do with something so small."

"You can go into Rapid City and see if the vet has anything." Josh looked up from the tiny kitten for a moment before focusing back on the little bundle.

"Come with me, please." Stone didn't want to miss out on a moment with Josh and if chauffeuring him around meant they'd be together, he'd do it with a smile. "To be honest, I can't drive and hold him at the same time, and I'm already worried if he'll make it."

He kept his wolf under wraps and his expression as neutral as possible and tried not to be insulted by the indecision crossing Josh's face.

"Okay, let me grab my knitting and we can go."

Stone huffed out the breath he'd been holding. "Thank you. I know you don't have any reason to trust me. I'm sorry for overwhelming you last night. I swear I won't touch you again unless you ask."

The small grin and nervous glance Josh gave him warmed Stone's heart. Whatever Josh had been exposed to in his life, Stone would try to make up for, including his own unintended fuck up. His whole focus in life lay in convincing his mate they were perfect for each other. And then he'd kill who ever put that terrified look on his mate's face.

Chapter Three

Josh's wolf stayed in the far recess of his mind for the entire drive to Rapid City. He worked on a knitting project during the drive. The rhythmic clicks soothed his nerves and burned off some of the nervous energy building inside him. The moment he sat in the cab of Stone's truck, the wild scent of pine trees and...ink? surrounded him. That wasn't a normal scent associated with wolves but a seductive undertone of something heady and luscious wrapped around his senses, commanding his attention. It tempted him to close the distance between them and reminded him of the first couple minutes of last night when he'd lost himself in Stone's kiss. Fifteen minutes in his presence and Josh started reconsidering his assumptions from last night.

Stone stayed true to his promise and didn't touch

him other than when he passed George over. The brief touch of their hands sent a tingle through Josh's entire body. He'd never felt so physically connected to another person in his life. Even with his mom, he'd sensed detachment and wondered if she deliberately held herself back all those years ago as a self-preservation habit.

"What are you making?"

Stone's question jarred Josh out of his reflection. He glanced down at his hands to remind himself which project he worked on. "I'm working on a pattern for a prayer shawl. It's all charted out, but I need to test knit one for display and to work out any mistakes in the pattern."

"You're very talented." Stone reached out with one hand and stroked along the edge of the shawl, but just before he reached Josh's fingers, he pulled his hand away. "It's very soft string."

"It's my favorite alpaca-merino blend. I've used it for a hundred different projects." The words tumbled out before Josh could stop them. Normally people's eyes glazed over when he started talking about yarn.

"It's nice. I'd like a sweater made out of it. Do you do custom work?"

No. The one word sat on the tip of Josh's tongue.

Every knitter knew the superstition behind making something big like a sweater for someone you were dating or had a crush on. The boyfriend curse would strike and the relationship would end before you finished the sweater. Does the curse extend to mates? Stone insisted he and Josh were mates but his wolf hadn't shown any extra interest in Stone. Considering the trauma they'd been treated to in the past, he understood his animal's preference for hiding.

"I do personal knitting. Gee asked me to make something for his daughter's birthday."

"Maybe when you're done, we could arrange something?" Stone gripped the steering wheel as he raced down the highway. "Is George okay?"

Josh lifted the edge of his sweater and peered down at the little creature. It twitched, which he took as a positive sign. "I think so. He's still with us."

"Good."

Stone didn't say anything more, but Josh could see he was truly worried about the kitten. He'd never known any dominant male to care so much about something so utterly helpless. It made him question his assumptions a little bit, but he'd been fooled before and was determined to protect himself. But he didn't kick the shit out of you for kneeing him in the balls.

He mentally winced at the memory. There'd been every chance for Stone to get payback but, instead, Stone chased him down and then kept him warm and protected all night. When Josh woke this morning, refreshed and warm, he realized he hadn't slept as soundly in years. Part of it had to be exhaustion, but he couldn't deny the security Stone's presence offered.

"Um, Stone, about last night?" Josh reached up and tugged on a couple of dreadlocks, trying to figure out the perfect way to say what he needed to without making the situation worse.

"Why don't we forget about last night?"

"But, I kneed you in the nuts."

Stone glanced over at him then shook his head. "Yeah, you did. But, I can't say I didn't deserve it. I didn't listen to you or pay attention to your reactions and I acted like a self-centered asshole. Next time, though, could you punch me in the chest or pinch me under the arm first?"

"Next time?" Josh didn't know whether to be thrilled or terrified. He couldn't deny an attraction to the big man. Physically, Stone encompassed everything that Josh had learned to fear, but his humor and patience created a crack in the wall Josh had built around himself.

"There will be a next time, Josh. I'm getting hard thinking about kissing you again."

Josh couldn't help it—he glanced down at Stone's lap and, sure enough, a thick ridge pressed up against his jeans. Saliva flooded his mouth, forcing him to swallow quickly or drool.

"Yup, and it's all yours, baby, as soon as you say the word."

"Really?" He didn't believe for a second Stone would truly wait until Josh made the first move. Dominants took what they wanted from omegas because they knew it was almost impossible for them to say no.

"I'm not saying I'm going to sit back and not encourage you, but you have my word I won't repeat last night. You set the pace and I'll move with you."

Stone never took his gaze off the road, but Josh suspected he watched him from his peripheral vision. Instead of continuing the conversation, he checked on little George, stroking a finger down the kitten's back. How would Stone react if the little guy didn't make it? Would he really care or was this all an act to lull him into a false sense of security?

"What do you do, Stone? Have you lived in Los Lobos your whole life?"

"I'm a tattoo artist. I used to live here but my parents packed us up and moved to Alaska in the middle of the night when I was six. At the time, I didn't understand why, but I've heard stories about the previous alpha and I'm glad they did it. I've always known I wanted to come back one day."

"Magnum Tao?" Josh turned and looked out the window, his fingers rhythmically working the stitches on the needles easing the anxiety he could feel building in his chest. A tattoo artist. That explains the ink scent.

"Drew's father, yes. My parents are accountants and not dominant in the least."

"How did you end up so big?"

"My dad is a big guy. You know size has nothing to do with dominance, right?"

"No." Josh shook his head. "Every dominant I've ever met has been bigger and stronger than everyone else." But I came from a small pack with little patience for submissives. "How long have you been tattooing?" It might not be the smoothest way to change topics, but Josh didn't want to look like a sheltered idiot.

57

"Twenty years, I've traveled all over the states and spent some time in Japan learning different styles and apprenticing." He reached down and rolled up his right sleeve. Josh's mouth watered at the sight of the rolled, checkered shirtsleeve over a muscular, tattooed arm. The wide leather and silver cuff on Stone's thick wrist sent tingles along Josh's spine and his cock twitched. He had no idea why but, damn, did it ever turn him on. Fuck, he's hot.

Stone turned his hand. Above the leather cuff, a beautiful koi fish swam up the inside of his arm. Josh moved before his brain could think. Reaching out, he stroked his fingers along the fish scales, expecting to feel the slight bumps from the tattoo. An insane urge to lick a path along the silky skin rocketed thought him. A quick mental check proved his inner wolf still cowered but was curious about his mate.

Josh pulled his hand back and resumed knitting, trying to ignore the burgeoning tension in the truck. Only instead of fear, the heady scent of their combined arousal mixed in the air. They didn't say anything more until they pulled up in front of the Canyon Lake Veterinary Hospital.

Josh passed George over to Stone and then followed him in. The wonderful staff treated their little guy like a prince, cooing over him and venting with Stone over the injustice of how he'd been tossed away. An hour later, they left with a bag full of supplies and a list of things they would need to take care of him over the next few weeks and in the future, because Stone already said he would keep him.

"She said there is a place called Pet Pantry on West Omaha where we can get everything." Josh tucked the little downy blanket in around George's sleeping form. His full, round belly gave him a healthier appearance.

Stone smiled down at him and Josh felt his heart skip a beat. "That's the first time you said we."

"Don't read too much into it." Josh looked down and averted his gaze. "They said he will need a lot of care until he gets a bit bigger." He didn't want Stone to think he planned to jump into anything with him, but he'd grown attached to George. Watching Stone fuss over the tiny creature, his protective instincts were obvious to anyone who knew what to look for. It wasn't surprising that Drew asked him to be one of the pack protectors.

Stone opened his door and supported his elbow as he hopped into the cab. When he didn't let go right away, Josh looked over at him. Sitting on the bench almost put Josh's face level with Stone's, and for a second he thought about closing the space between them. Kiss me.

Stone winked and shut the door. Josh fought the urge to growl in frustration and tried to ignore the disappointment surging through him. Stone kept to his word, only now Josh questioned if he wanted him to.

It only took a few minutes to reach the Pet Pantry, and Josh passed George over to Stone to carry again. The vet had suggested they restrict how much George was handled. In Stone's big hand, it looked like he carried a balled-up towel.

"What collar should we get him?" Stone stood in front of a massive display of leashes and collars in all shapes, sizes, and colors.

Josh pressed his lips together and fought the urge to snicker at the big softie. "I don't think we have to worry about it until he gets a little bigger. He's practically the size of a peanut right now. You can always come back in a few weeks and pick one out when you get to know his personality."

"Good idea. We can come back later." Stone arched his eyebrow as if daring Josh to argue with him. If he had been anyone else, he might have agreed, but since it was Stone, he simply rolled his eyes and continued on. They made it a few more feet before Stone stopped in front of the cat toys and started analyzing each of them. Josh continued on to the next aisle, picking up the immediate necessities.

"I thought I saw you coming in here. What do you need in a pet store, Joshie? Your dad has a pretty pink collar for you as soon as we get your ass home."

Josh's chest seized at the sound of Donnovan's best friend. Eddie's nasally voice had always made his skin crawl. He turned and looked down the aisle. Eddie stood leaning against the shelves, his black hair combed back like a greaser from the 1960s. Josh knew a lack of washing and general personal hygiene created the look.

"Donnovan is not my father." He wished his voice didn't shake and he shared the powerful depth of Stone's confidence.

"Doesn't matter, fag. You have something of his and he wants it back."

"I don't know what you're talking about."

"Bullshit. Don't worry, I don't even want it." He took a step closer, forcing Josh to step back. "I want to bring you back so he gets his pound of flesh for your disrespectful actions, after I kick your cock-loving ass."

The putrid stench of his breath made Josh want to gag, but before Eddie could follow through with any threats, he suddenly disappeared. Stone appeared between them. "Hold George," he snarled before gently laying the bundle in the basket Josh carried.

"Who the fuck are you to come into this territory without asking my alpha's permission?"

"Hey, dude." Eddie lifted his hands. "I'm merely passing through. Saw Joshie here and thought I'd stop and say hi. I'm a friend of his father, known the kid almost his whole life."

"He's not my father," Josh whispered as defiantly as he could. He didn't know if anyone had heard him until Stone reached back and patted the side of his hip.

"Funny, it sounded like you were threatening one of my pack members on pack land."

"Rapid City isn't pack land."

Josh winced at Eddie's tone. He remembered the belligerent tone and knew it meant the sneaky bastard already planned something.

"Try me." Stone's quiet tone didn't change. He didn't get loud or growl, but Josh could feel the anger radiating off of him. "Get in your piece of shit vehicle and continue on your way before I bring your sorry ass to Alpha Tao."

"Heard Drew's a pussy compared to his old man." Stone didn't move a muscle at the insult. The dominants from Josh's old pack would have attacked and torn Eddie to shreds for an insult to their alpha. When he heard Eddie start to walk away, he risked a peek around Stone's arm. The evil bastard stared right at him, his lip curled in a defiant sneer. "Looks like pussies attract more pussies or cocksuckers in this case. See you around, Joshie."

"No, you won't." Stone shifted his weight and blocked Josh's view. As soon as Josh realized Eddie had left the building, the shakes settled into his arms. His wolf retreated so far back in his head, he could hardly feel him.

"Give me the basket, Josh." Stone wrapped his fingers over his, and he forced himself to unclench his fingers as Stone scooped the basket out of his hands.

"I have to leave." He should have known better than to come here. He'd been caught up in fantasies of a long lost family who would welcome him with open arms. Instead, he found out his mother's family were a bunch of assholes who'd turned their back on their daughter when she left. He should have known Donnovan would have thought about the Black Hills pack and assigned someone to watch out for him.

"Look at me, Josh."

Unable to deny the command in Stone's voice, he lifted his head and gazed at the row of buttons bisecting his denim shirt.

"Up higher, Josh. Look at my face."

It took him a minute to work up the courage to meet Stone's eyes. He'd been slapped down more times than he could count for meeting Donnovan's gaze. But Stone's features didn't show any vicious superiority. If anything, Josh thought he saw relief softening the edges of his jawline.

"That's better. I'm not going to allow anything to happen to you. We're going to pay for this stuff and then take George home."

Josh focused on damage control. His one act of defiance would haunt him for the rest of his life. *I never should have taken Donnovan's ring.* "You can have my shop. I'm moving on."

"No, you're not making any decisions until we talk to Drew and Ryker."

At the mention of Ryker's name fear coursed through Josh. He'd never met the man but he'd seen him once coming out of Drew's office. The enforcer projected everything in dominants that scared the hell out of him. "No, I'll go and not cause any more trouble."

"Shhh." Stone pulled Josh closer and he went willingly. Memories sifted past the rampant panic, reminding him of how safe he'd been last night. "You're safe, baby. Take a nice deep breath for me, slowly to the count of four, and then I want you to breathe out just as slow.

He did as Stone asked, breathing in and out as he counted. Gradually, his heart rate slowed to almost normal, and his throat didn't feel like it was closing up on him.

"Good, boy." He rubbed Josh's back and pressed a gentle kiss to the top of his head. "Okay, let's get George home first. We can talk in the truck about what you need."

Josh nodded, his hands still shook but not as bad as when he held onto the basket. "Is George okay? Did I hurt him?"

"He's fine, still sleeping. Why don't you hold him while I pay for this stuff?"

Stone placed the bundle in his hands, and Josh risked a peek under the corner of the towel. George looked the same as he did when they left the clinic, sleeping peacefully in the knowledge he was safe. *I'll never know the feeling.* Before he realized it, Stone tucked him up under his arm and led him out of the store. He blinked, thinking they hadn't paid, except Stone now carried a large shopping bag. *I'm losing it.*

He moved wherever Stone led, despite the rampant urge to take off and run away before he made things any worse. Stone exuded a sense of security Josh craved right now. *Until the day he turns on me.* The thought ricocheted around his mind. He truly believed dominants couldn't be trusted, but for the first time an element of his beliefs didn't sit right with him. Was it fair to assume Stone would be like every other dominant he'd met before? *Except for Gee. He might be brusque, but he didn't threaten me even when I flirted with him. Drew, too, hadn't done anything to intimidate him,* if he remembered correctly, his alpha promised to keep him safe. Fighting a panic attack while in the presence of a man who could order his death clouded his memories of the meeting and prevented him from remembering everything Drew said.

The Black Hills pack was very different from the pack he grew up in. Maybe it was time he started believing in what he'd seen and experienced. Nothing had happened, outside of his own fears, that would prove he was in danger. It certainly was something to contemplate. Josh focused on the scenery passing by the window and realized they were already over halfway back to Los Lobos. He glanced over at Stone who looked ready to murder someone. His fingers gripped the wheel so tight, Josh wondered if it would snap. Stone's jaw looked like it had been carved from granite, and Josh could make out the rhythmic flexing of a muscle in his neck. Fear carved into his psyche, an old habit born of a hundred backhands by pissed off enforcers. Stone's nose twitched slightly before he snapped his head to the side, pinning Josh with his eyes. They'd gone primal and he could see Stone's wolf in his gaze.

"You're back." Stone reached over and wrapped his fingers around Josh's hand where it lay on the seat between them. "You scared the hell out of me."

"I didn't go anywhere. I'm sorry." Josh didn't know how to respond to Stone's comments and when he pulled the truck to the side of the road, Josh automatically tensed up, waiting for the first strike.

Stone put the truck in park, left the engine running then reached over and unbuckled Josh, hauling him across the bench seat into his lap.

Josh sat perfectly still, completely confused by Stone's actions. As the moments passed, the heat of Stone's chest seeped past the icy, frightened shell he'd wrapped himself in. Even his wolf crawled out of hiding a little bit, frightened but curious of the immense sense of security vibrating against him.

"Relax, Josh. Let me hold you for a minute."

"Why?"

"Why? Because you phased out. I tried talking to you and you wouldn't answer. You were comatose, but your body kept moving wherever I directed you. All your lights were on but nobody was home." Stone stroked his hand up and down Josh's arm. Lulled by the rhythmic movement, the tension melted Josh's muscles. "I knew you were scared, but when you wouldn't respond to me I started to freak. The guy in the store, he's the one who abused you, isn't he? What did he do to you?"

Stone's voice dropped an octave with the last question and Josh realized he battled his wolf. A soft light came on in the darkness where his wolf hid as they both understood Stone wouldn't lash out at them. He was suppressing his wolf so Josh didn't become more upset.

68

"He's a friend of my stepfather. They do favors for each other, and I think Eddie must owe him big because he will do anything Donnovan says."

"Donnovan is your stepfather?"

"Yes, Eddie used me as a punching bag before to vent his anger but not for a long time. I ran away twelve years ago, after my mom died." A shudder quaked along his spine and Stone held him tighter, pressing a kiss on top of his head.

"It's okay, I swear he'll never touch you again."

"I know because I'm going to leave." Josh rubbed his cheek against Stone's soft beard before ducking and resting his cheek on Stone's shoulder.

"No, we're going to talk to Drew and Ryker before you make any big decisions."

"Stone, I'm no one. Just a useless, frightened omega who isn't brave enough to stand up to anyone. George is braver than I am for Pete's sake." He felt weak, frightened, and wanted to curl up somewhere and hide. "Where is George?"

"I put him in the carrier on the backseat." Josh didn't remember buying one but then he didn't remember much after Eddie's appearance. Stone lifted him up and slid him onto the seat next to him. Wrapping an arm around him, he tucked Josh up

69

next to him.

"What are you doing?"

"I'm doing what's right and not trying to vent my frustration by kissing you senseless."

"I've never heard of that technique." Josh looked behind him and saw the sturdy-looking cat carrier resting on the seat. "Usually a fist is better for venting."

A deep, angry growl rumbled in Stone's throat and the air seized in Josh's throat. He glanced over at Stone who looked out the windshield like he planned to run someone over. He fought the urge to slide across the seat away from him.

"Did I say something wrong?"

"Don't talk about being abused like it's normal or acceptable. It makes me want to turn this truck around, hunt the fucker down, and tear him apart with my bare hands."

Josh glanced up at Stone who concentrated on checking his mirrors before pulling the truck back out onto the road. Stone caught him and smiled before pecking a quick kiss on his forehead. "I know we've gotten off on a bit of a rocky start, Josh, but I've already learned a lot about you. First and most important, you are one of the bravest people I've met."

"You're delusional." Josh could accept being described as creative and kind, but he didn't have a courageous bone in his body.

"Nope, not at all. In fact I'm thinking clearer than I have since I left Alaska." He pulled the truck out onto the road and continued to Los Lobos.

Josh waited for Stone to say something more, but silence hung in the vehicle until he couldn't stand it any longer. "Why do you think I'm brave?"

"The real question should be: why don't you believe you're brave?"

Josh stared out the window at the road ahead of them, his mind circling around the question. He could list a hundred reasons why he knew he lacked that particular trait. What he wanted to know is why did Stone think he possessed it?

"I don't understand this game, Stone."

"It's not a game, Josh. If I'm going to have a chance at winning you, then you need to accept you are worth being wanted. I'm willing to bet you never considered finding a mate one day, did you?"

No, in fact he never had. Why would anyone want weak, sniveling, cowardly Joshie for a mate?

"Why did you leave your old pack?"

"Because, I'm nothing but a useless omega who's only good use is as a whipping boy for everyone."

Another growl rumbled in Stone's throat but it didn't frighten Josh as much this time. Stone was simply a vocal guy. Would he be this vocal during sex? The question flashed through his mind and didn't go away. For the first time in...well, forever, Josh wanted to find out what it would be like to go to bed with a big strong man.

"So because of the abuse they heaped on you, you packed up and left. Where did you go?"

No one had ever asked Josh so many questions about himself, forcing him to recall memories he'd buried a long time ago. "I wandered, lived on the streets in survival mode. I wouldn't really call it a life." He told Stone about Mrs. Arven and how she taught him to knit and gave him a room in exchange for helping her around the shop and odd jobs at home.

"So not only were you brave enough to get out of an abusive situation, you lived on your own and then trusted a complete stranger...and you honestly think you're not brave?"

He sat there and watched the trees pass through the window. Potholes and uneven trails made the road into Los Lobos brutal. Josh had made the trip one way but didn't know if his little car would survive navigating its way out. The truck bounced around at the speed Stone drove. "No...I hid. I wasn't brave. I did what I had to, to save my ass."

"There are a lot of people who would have curled up and accepted their lot in life and never done anything to change it. You did. That takes immense courage." Stone slid his hand up Josh's far arm until he cupped the side of his head, pulling him closer to his body in a side hug. "I'm proud of you for saving yourself. I might have never found you otherwise."

Josh wanted to believe him, but there were so many things pointing toward the opposite of bravery. He kept his arms wrapped around his chest, holding himself, when all he really wanted to do was wrap around Stone and beg him to protect him. "Don't put me on any pedestal. Eddie found me; my ass is back to being grass. I can't bring that kind of trouble here, not when the town is still rebuilding."

Stone leaned down and nuzzled the top of his head. "We've all done stupid things in life, myself included. I swear to you the asshole will never touch a single hair on your head. We'll be back in Los Lobos soon and then we can talk about the future." George made a little bit of noise, drawing their attention. "First we need to feed this little guy again and get him settled. The vet said he'll need to be fed at least every two hours. We have to keep him warm and hydrated."

"You can drop me off at the shop and I'll meet you at your place if you like."

"Nope. I'm sticking to you like glue, baby."

Yes! Josh couldn't deny the relief pouring through him with the knowledge he wouldn't be alone. It might not be fair to dump his problems at Stone's feet, but he craved the feeling of safety in his arms. "Why bother?"

"Because, I know how brave you are and you have already admitted to making stupid choices sometimes. I'm going to make sure you don't make another one by taking off on me before we get a chance to talk."

Josh would have been insulted if it wasn't true. He'd already thought George would make a good distraction and ease his escape. It felt good to know someone cared, even if the idea of getting involved terrified him.

Chapter Four

Josh didn't say a single word for the rest of the drive back to town. Stone wondered if he'd pissed off his mate by essentially inviting himself into his home or if he'd been right about Josh getting ready to run. The intriguing scent of lanolin and prey continued to cycle around desperation and fear. The one silver lining in the dark cloud was the soft, delicate arousal tickling his senses every once in a while. Stone clung to the knowledge that Josh felt the attraction brewing between them.

Desperate to connect with the animal side of his mate, Stone's wolf paced back and forth in his head. He'd never met another wolf like Josh or one with his talent for maintaining his humanity. Even when he'd been terrified by the asshole in the pet shop, his wolf never surfaced to protect him. Stone didn't know many omegas, but even the gentlest wolf should snarl when cornered. Josh's wolf must have been beaten into extreme submission; it was the only logical explanation. Stone's heart broke, making him wish he'd torn Eddie apart when he had the chance.

There would be another opportunity and it pacified his wolf for the moment. He'd known many "Eddies" over the years, stupid wolves happy to follow orders when it suited their own sick, depraved needs. They craved perversion and violence, and Stone didn't lose a moment's sleep over the few he'd challenged and killed.

Keeping Josh tucked close to his side went a long way toward calming his wolf. He liked the softness of Josh's thin dreadlocks and couldn't wait to grip them when he claimed his sweet ass. His mate might be distracted by his thoughts at the moment, but Stone was hyperaware of every part of his body touching him. A plan for how he could seduce his mate and hopefully entice his wolf out of hiding began to form.

"Stone, why did you come to the shop last night?"

Damn, shitty timing. He'd wanted to put his seduction plan into action before Josh remembered to ask about last night. "I'd mentioned to Drew I wanted to buy your building."

"And I ruined your plans."

"No, not it at all." He didn't want to give Josh any excuse to leave. "I'd be lying if I said I wasn't disappointed, but then Drew mentioned you might not need the entire store space for your string."

"It's yarn."

"Right, Yarn. I'd planned to ask if you would be interested in renting out part of the building. The moment you opened the door, my whole world changed."

"Oh." Josh fell silent again, relaxing against Stone's side. His wolf settled, knowing his mate was so close. Wrapping his arm across Josh's shoulder, he steadied him while navigating the treacherous road into town. They were just pulling up in front of the building when Josh spoke again.

"Do you need special plumbing or anything?"

"Nope, a sink and electrical." Stone's heart jumped a beat at the prospect of having his own place so close to his mate's.

"Oh." Josh didn't say anything more and Stone didn't press him.

Stone didn't believe they would be in any real danger in the middle of town, but it didn't stop him from scanning the immediate area and scenting the breeze for any potential danger to Josh or George. It didn't take them long to get everything unpacked and inside.

"Don't forget to set the locks behind us."

"Got it." He turned the dead bolt on the main door and then locked the door at the bottom of the stairs. There were two deadbolts and a chain attached to the lower door. At the top of the stairs there were another two deadbolts and a chain on the door to his apartment. Stone didn't see the point to the extra locks when the doors were flimsy enough any shifter could tear them off. He kept his comments to himself because he didn't want to destroy Josh's fragile sense of security. With Stone here now, nothing would get at his mate anyway.

The apartment spanned the entire upper floor, and it looked very cozy despite the lack of furniture. The ceiling angled in to a point above them but it was high enough he didn't worry about whacking his head. Gleaming hardwood floors extended the length of the main room. A small kitchen sat off to the right side, with a futon sofa on the floor with a TV across from it. A large basket overflowed with balls of yarn and what looked like unfinished projects sat next to it. A pile of folded afghans was tucked on the shelf of the end table. Two doorways sat open—one led to a bathroom and the other exposed a bedroom with a bed. Relief swept through him as he'd been worried Josh slept on the futon.

While Stone looked around the room, Josh got the formula ready for George before moving to sit on the futon. He propped the kitten up with his hand like the vet showed them. Needing to do something, Stone popped open the clips on the carrier and put the lid to the side. "We can use this as a little bed for him until he's older. Where do you want to keep it?"

George chewed at the nipple of the little bottle, formula dripping from the corner of the kitten's mouth as he sucked it down. "In here," Josh replied. "There is a bit of a draft in my room, which I don't mind but could be dangerous for him.

"I'll tuck the heating pad on one side of the carrier." Stone rearranged the blankets in the carrier, making a nest for the tiny kitten. "It'll keep him warm but also allow him to crawl a few inches to get away if he gets uncomfortable."

It didn't take George long to finish his meal and flop to one side like a drunken sailor. Josh tucked him into his little nest, sound asleep.

The simmering tension between them bubbled up. Before Josh could change his mind, Stone took the lead. "Come here." He tugged his mate closer; pulling him up into his arms he kissed Josh on the forehead and then pressed his lips to his mate's temple. His wolf pressed against his consciousness, demanding more, insisting on claiming the gentle wolf, but Stone kept a tight grip on his primal side. He refused to overwhelm and scare Josh again. He'd promised to go at Josh's pace and he'd do it if it killed him.

"What are you doing, Stone?"

"Kissing you."

"You missed my lips by about two inches."

"Everyone kisses on the lips." He pecked a kiss on the end of Josh's nose. "I like to be different."

Josh looked up at him and Stone held his gaze. His eyes were the color of milk chocolate and so full of expression, even if he couldn't scent Josh's emotions, he'd be able to read them in his eyes. "You are so beautiful." He slid the back of his finger along the edge of his dreadlocks, skimming along the side of his face and jaw. When Josh went to lower his head in an obviously submissive move, Stone traced his finger along his chin and stopped him. "There aren't any challenges between us. You're my mate. My equal."

"I am nowhere near equal to you."

"You sure as hell are. I'll give you a list. Number

one, your eyes are much prettier than mine. Number two, you're much more graceful than I am. You can run through the forest at top speed and hardly disturb anything. Me, I'm like a bull in a china shop."

"Yeah, well you could tear me in two."

"But, you could tear my heart in two."

"Oh." Josh's eyes softened and Stone almost pumped his fist in the air. *See, baby, I can be romantic.* He made a mental note to look up how to do romantic shit on the Internet so he could keep the soft look on his mate's face. Suddenly the rumbling of an empty stomach rose between them.

"Was that George?" Stone asked, making Josh laugh. He loved the way his nose crinkled up when he smiled. "Hungry?"

"Starving," he replied. "I don't have much here. I went to Gee's last night because I'd planned to get some groceries today.

"You were at Gee's last night?" *No wonder I kept smelling prey and everyone thought I was nuts.*

"Yeah, why?"

"I rented a room from Gee last night. I must have just missed you." He slid his fingers along Josh's neck, loving the feel of his soft skin. "How about I run down to the diner and pick us up something to eat?"

"As long as you don't mind sitting on the floor. I don't have a kitchen table."

"You make us a nest while I'm out." He took a chance and pressed a quick kiss against Josh's lips. He meant to keep it short and sweet, but the moment their lips met, he wanted more. Thankfully Josh didn't seem in any big hurry to end it. His tongue tentatively lapped at Stone's bottom lips and he welcomed the chance to deepen their kiss. This time, though, he paid close attention to Josh's reactions and let him set the pace. After what seemed like a brief moment in time, Josh's stomach grumbled again. Stone slowly ended their kiss, rotating his hips so he could press his aching cock against Josh's hip. Only a couple of inches separated them in height which Stone thought was perfect.

"Goddamn you kiss like a dream, baby." His voice sounded rough to him, the low grumble an echo of his wolf demanding more. "You can kiss me any time you want."

Josh grinned, his cheeks a soft pink from Stone's whiskers. He reached out to touch his cheek. "They didn't hurt you did they?" He'd kept a short beard since his teenage years but if it irritated Josh's skin, he'd make the sacrifice.

"No, I like the way it feels." Josh rubbed his fingers against Stone's beard. "It's softer than it looks."

Stone knew he needed to leave now or risk pressing Josh for more. He wanted them naked and wrestling on the bed he saw in the other room, but keeping his promise was more important. It didn't mean he couldn't tease and seduce a few more kisses before the night ended. Leaning down, he kissed the skin below Josh's ear. "Just imagine how good it will feel against your balls."

Josh's gasp was the perfect response; his red cheeks were adorable. Letting him go, Stone headed for the stairs. "Lock the door behind me, baby. I'll be back in about twenty minutes."

***

Josh paced back and forth across the room debating the pros and cons of inviting Stone to stay with him. We could have sex, that's a pro. Josh didn't bother lying to himself by pretending he didn't feel any attraction to the man, but fear and attraction continued to battle for supremacy in his head. If he said a definitive no, Stone would've backed down.

He hadn't retaliated for the pain Josh had caused him the previous night, so it didn't make any sense why he continued to be frightened? Because if we allow him to come close and he get violent, it would break my heart and mind forever. Something so frightening Josh didn't want to contemplate it. He wanted to believe Stone was his knight in shining armor, but in his personal experience, the strong always preyed on the weak.

Needing the distraction, he quickly got out some cutlery and plates. Grabbing takeout didn't mean they had to eat out of a box. He set everything out on the kitchen counter, checked on George, and then moved close enough to the window to watch for Stone, but not so close anyone looking would see him.

As soon as he spotted Stone approaching, he unlocked all the doors and opened the shop door to let him in. Five minutes later they were both on his small sofa eating in a companionable silence. Stone rolled up his shirt sleeves again and the thick leather and silver band on his wrist kept drawing Josh's attention. He'd never considered wrists to be particularly sexy, but Stone's seemed to be the exception.

"Do you regret any of yours?" The question shot out of Josh's mouth before he could rethink it. Stone's complicated tattooed sleeve fascinated him, an eclectic collection of Japanese influence with dragons, koi fish, and a darker edge with skulls and demonic eyes peering from the shadows. The mixture of color with black and white captivated and inspired Josh to put together some complicated stitches and design a shawl. His groups would love a badass shawl mimicking tattoos around their arms when they wore it. He might not ever be brave enough to get a tattoo for himself, but he'd happily wrap an ink-inspired shawl around him. Especially in the wintertime when the temperature drops to disgusting lows.

Thankfully, Stone didn't appear fazed by his obscure question. He shrugged as he chewed the food in his mouth, swallowing before speaking. "I have a couple that if I had to do them again I might change it up a bit, but for the most part I'm happy with my ink. There are some special memories other people might not understand, but they are my memories on my skin for me and not for anyone else. A lot of the ones on my legs are from when I practiced on myself."

He lifted Josh's empty plate from his hands. "I'll

do the dishes."

Josh followed Stone into the tiny kitchen, needing to be close to the big man who equally scared and intrigued him. "What kind of memories? Most of your art looks very intimidating and scary; did you have a difficult childhood?" Josh could understand and sympathize. His had been day after day of a never-ending nightmare. Until the day he realized he could survive on his own and the streets were a better choice.

"I had a very normal childhood, no matter what society might think of my appearance. This one is my favorite." He lifted his T-shirt, baring his skin.

Stone might have wanted Josh to look at a tattoo, but the muscular ridges across his stomach distracted him. "Fuck, I could do my laundry on those." Before he could stop himself, Josh reached out to touch Stone's chest.

His skin felt hot under Josh's fingertips, as he slowly caressed the outline of the muscular abs. An electrical shimmer of awareness and need washed over him, tempting him to touch more, to trace each of Stone's divine stomach muscles and then slip them lower, below his waistband.

"The tattoo is a little higher, little one." Stone took

a deep breath in, and Josh could feel the shudder in his breath and the shiver on his skin as he slid his hand over the man's stomach and waist. When Stone moved closer, Josh realized he'd been practically petting the big man.

"Oh God. I'm sorry." He pulled away as if Stone's skin had scalded him. What the hell is wrong with me? Bad boys have a reputation for a reason. I'm going to end up on the wrong end of a fist again.

Stone grabbed his hand and pressed it back against his abs. "Keep it there." Stone pulled his T-shirt off over his head, baring his entire torso. "I like the way your hand feels on me."

Josh feared his heart might pound right out of his rib cage. No matter what the small frightened voice in his head said, he couldn't bring himself to move away. Stone's chest wasn't as hairy as Josh expected, but the fine strands tickled his fingertips, enticing him to do more. Touching Stone reminded him of stroking rich alpaca, captivating and sensual. He didn't see the incredible artistry that had been inked into him as he focused on the skin under his palm. His inner wolf uncharacteristically yanked at his senses. He wanted to run, be hunted, and then caught. Oh, yeah, getting caught would be the best part.

Stone reached down and caught his other hand, bringing the fist up to his face. He gently kissed the back of each knuckle, before sliding his finger under, encouraging Josh to relax. When he did, Stone wrapped his lips around each digit, swirling his tongue around the digit before drawing it into his hot, wet mouth. Josh's knees almost buckled at the gentle suction on each of his fingers. A sensual thread attached to each digit led straight to his cock. Every swirl and suck echoed down to the flesh between his legs.

"What are you doing?" It might be a stupid question even to Josh's ears, but he couldn't formulate a coherent thought with Stone's tongue against his skin.

"Tasting you...."

A nervous laugh escaped him. "You planning on eating me?"

"I plan on licking and nibbling on every inch of your sweet body." Stone's eye shifted glowing amber, his pupils dilating until Josh could see the wolf in his gaze. Unlike last night, the fear didn't overwhelm him. "It's up to you when it happens."

His heart skipped a beat or two while he looked up

into Stone's eyes. The heat in his gaze seared past the wall of fear building up in his brain. Is one day long enough to trust him? What if he's setting me up, or sucking me in?

The mental excuses sounded lame even to him. "What if I want you now?"

"Do you really?"

Josh nodded his head so quickly his neck might as well have been made of rubber.

"Tell me what you want."

Josh licked his lips, his mouth dried, his heart racing fast enough to cause a heart attack. "I want you."

"Be specific, I don't want to push you farther than you're willing to go right now."

"To be honest, I'm kind of curious about exactly how your beard would feel on my balls."

Stone chuckled, drawing Josh closer into his embrace. He didn't let go, instead laid Josh's palm over his heart and trapped it there with his own hand. Josh could feel the strong, rapid beat of Stone's heart under his palm.

"Your heart is beating fast," Josh said timidly. "As if you're nervous."

"I am nervous, Josh. Frightening you is the last

thing I want to do. I'm fucking aching for you and I'm so incredibly afraid of overwhelming you."

No one ever held themselves back for Josh. In every sexual encounter he'd participated in, his partner never put his feelings or needs first. It empowered him and fed his courage. "Would you kiss me fir—?"

Stone's mouth swooped down on his, his lips gentle and teasing, but the intensity in the room skyrocketed. He reached around and cupped Josh's ass with one hand, squeezing and massaging one cheek as he kept the other hand anchored over his heart.

Hard enough to pound nails, Josh rocked against the thick rod pressing into his hips proved Stone's arousal matched his. Stone licked the roof of his mouth and sucked on his tongue. He might as well have been working his cock as waves of intense pleasure throbbed along his veins, matching his heartbeat. When he moaned and rocked his cock against Stone's thigh, the kiss ended.

"Are you okay, Josh?" Stone sounded as if he'd run ten miles at top speed and his heart pounded like a heavy-metal drummer under his palm.

"Come into the bedroom."

"I'll follow you anywhere, baby." Stone flopped down on the bed on his back. "Come crawl over me, gorgeous." Josh reached for the bed, pausing when Stone held up his hand, a naughty grin curling up the corners of his lips. "Naked."

Josh gnawed at his lower lip for a moment as the big man pushed himself up, reclining back on his elbows to watch him strip. He took a deep, cleansing breath before tugging his sweater over his head. Any insecurity he might have felt about his slim body burned away under Stone's scalding look.

Stone braced himself on one arm, reaching down to unbutton his jeans and blatantly rub the thick ridge under the fabric. "Don't tease, baby. Let me see some more."

Feeling sexy and very much a tease, Josh slowly unzipped his cargo pants, letting them hang precariously on his hips as he stretched up his arms. Stone rolled over and twisted, lying across the bed on his stomach. "Come over here; let me touch you. I'll be good, just my mouth."

Josh slowly moved forward, swinging his hips, feeling as powerful as a god. His pants dropped down and he kicked them off and to the side. His bed was the perfect height because Stone's face sat just below his cock. True to his word he gripped the bed spread as he nuzzled Josh's cock through his underwear.

"Take them off for me, please. I'll rub my beard on your balls."

Nothing in the universe could have stopped Josh from giving in to Stone's growled request. His voice had dropped a couple of octaves and his eyes were all wolf, but he still kept his hands to himself.

Josh bared himself, kicking the last fragment of fabric away. His cock bobbed, rigid and flushed, as he freed it. Stone growled low in his throat and reached for Josh before snatching his hand back. "Fuck, I'm trying to keep my promise." Tucking his hands under his chest he lifted himself, moving his mouth level with Josh's cock. "Closer, baby. Rub your sweet cock against my beard...."

Nothing could have prepared him for the first brush of Stone's whiskers against his cock. He expected it to prickle, but it felt more like a silky pelt tickling his skin. He wanted Stone to rub his beard all over his balls, his cock, his entire body. For a moment, he got lost in the sensation and then had to pinch the base of his cock so as not to come like a teenager. "You win. More, I need more." He rubbed his length over Stone's jaw, pausing to swipe the tip over his lush lips. Both of them groaned at the contact, and a heartbeat later Josh's cock was encompassed by a hot, wet mouth. Stone didn't tease or play around. He slurped on Josh's dick like a melting ice cream cone, swirling his tongue around the length before engulfing him right to his balls. Josh gripped Stone's hair. The long, silky strands flowed over his fingers like water, adding another delicious layer of sensation.

Time seemed to stand still and the universe closed in around the two of them. No one ever took this much care with him...made him feel so special. A simple blow job never brought him such an acute rush of pleasure. Stone made love to his cock. Blow jobs were quick, dirty, with a single result, but Stone made certain Josh felt every nuance of his teasing, making him crave more. When Stone swallowed, his throat muscles massaged Josh's length in the best possible way, and he lost the battle with his own control. Snapping his hips with shallow jabs, he fucked Stone's mouth. Stone encouraged him with moans vibrating down to his balls until Josh lost this first passionate battle. The orgasmic bliss surged through his body over and over. Stone didn't miss a beat, licking and cleaning him up.

Josh's legs might as well have been made of gelatin, they shook so much. In a blink, he found himself scooped up and flipped over onto his stomach. The ease in which Stone moved him startled him, attesting to the excessive strength in his body.

"Lube," Stone snarled into his ear, and Josh pointed at the drawer in the small table next to the bed. Stone's incredible blow job stole his ability to think or rationalize. He hadn't planned to come down his throat, but couldn't help himself.

The snick of the cap opening drew Josh's attention. Stone would be annoyed and Josh feared he wouldn't take a few minutes to prepare him before fucking him. It had been such a long time and there was no way he could take a dense, thick cock right now. Instinctive fear burned away the lingering pleasure from his orgasm. It won't last long, maybe a few minutes, and it will be over. I can do it. "I'm sorry for not warning you before I came."

Stone prowled over top of him, pressing him into the bed. "Never apologize for that. You are hot as fuck, baby. I'm desperate to be inside you. If I get you ready, can you ride me?"

Josh looked over his shoulder, shocked. Not only was Stone not angry, but he offered to lie back and be ridden. "Do you mean it?"

A cold trickle seeped into the crack of his ass. "I've never meant anything more." Stone toyed with his anus, circling the entrance and dipping in and out, working the lube in farther and farther. Kissing a man while he finger fucked his ass might rank as the most erotic event Josh ever been treated to. Stone took his time, stretching and massaging his rear opening. By the time he worked up to three digits, Josh didn't care how much it burned. He wanted to feel his ass filled with Stone's cock.

Stone rolled onto his back and Josh followed, straddling his hips with his knees. His fingers circled around Stone's cock pointing it up for him to impale. Stone reached up and gripped the sheets over his head. "Whenever you're ready."

He lowered himself down on the rigid length beneath him. Tipping his head back, he closed his eyes and willed his body to relax. Stone's blunt tip pushed past the first ring of muscles, and Josh's breath caught at the exquisite perfection. Taking Stone's cock in with short little strokes and then a long push, he gasped for air.

"Look at me, baby, you okay?"

Josh opened his eyes and looked down at Stone,

his ass so freaking full he wasn't certain he'd ever be able to take a deep breath again. With the burn came the electric shivers of excitement. "Fuck, you feel so good." He shifted his hips slightly and Stone growled deep in his throat. The sound might as well have been a physical stroke along his senses because his cock jerked and his balls drew up tighter. "Oh, yeah. Do that again please."

"Oh, no, baby. You're not running away with this." Stone wrapped his fingers around Josh's sac and gave it a precise tug. The sharp jolt helped bring him back from leaping over the end into an orgasm, but at the same time ramped it up even higher.

"You're going to wait for me, Josh. I want to watch you as you come, but I want to be reaming your ass while you do." Stone wrapped his hand around the base of Josh's cock and squeezed.

"How do you know how to touch me?" Josh dug his fingers into the thick muscles layered over Stone's chest. "You're so fucking hard everywhere."

"And one way that really counts?"

"Oh God, yeah." Josh swirled his hips and Stone's eyes rolled up into his head.

"Fuck, do it again, baby."

Josh repeated the movement and Stone arched his

back before pushing up with a snap of his hips. "Again," he demanded and Josh happily complied. Every time he swirled his butt Stone would slide out ever so slightly and then snap his hips back up, driving the hot marble rod of a cock deep into his ass and pegging Josh's prostate over and over.

Their impromptu dance continued; neither one of them wanted to rush. Josh continually fought the urge to bounce like a fucking bunny. The need to feel Stone claim his ass rode him hard. His neck itched and his skin felt tight with anticipation. Bite me.

"I'm not putting my teeth near your beautiful neck tonight, Josh."

Josh blinked not realizing his eyes had closed or he'd spoken out loud. Looking down, he focused on Stone's intense expression below him. The burning light in Stone's eyes and the thickness of the cock he rode...he would have thought his feelings were all one-sided. Disappointment pierced his giddiness, "I thought...."

"Not this time, baby. I'm going to claim you one day. You're my mate, but I want to hear you beg for it."

"That's a little high-handed." Josh braced his hand on Stone's thick chest and raised his ass, dropping down on Stone's length.

Stone's expression darkened slightly and an icy claw of fear danced down Josh's spine.

Stone immediately grabbed his hips, pulling him down as he ground his pelvis up. "You want me but you're afraid. I get it. I'm not going to claim you until I'm convinced you're ready and until I see unconditional acceptance in your beautiful eyes I'm going to make you.... Wait. For. It." He punctuated each word with a quick jerk, pegging Josh's sweet spot.

His legs started to shake with the exertion of being spread wide while bobbing over his lover's body. Between one heartbeat and another, Stone rolled them over, flipping Josh's legs up over his arms until they rested against his shoulders.

"My mate." He drew the length of his cock out to the crown before stuffing it back in one long, constant stroke.

"Oh fuck." Josh grabbed Stone's forearms where they were braced on either side of his torso. This angle allowed him to push his cock deeper. Josh's ass burned like wildfire but the pleasure coursing along with it overshadowed any true pain.

"That's right. I'm fucking you. Think about that,

baby. Think about me biting the sensitive spot on your neck and claiming you for the rest of our lives. You are my sweet little mate and nothing will ever hurt you as long as I'm around."

But what about when you're gone? It would be only a matter of time before Stone left him, tossed him aside like everyone else in his life. Reality could be a nasty bitch and he wished she'd stayed away for a little longer and let him enjoy the moment.

"Stop thinking and feel." Stone pistoned in and out, driving Josh higher and higher up the bed. "You're mine to protect, even from your own negative thoughts."

He knew Stone scented the change in his thoughts.

A sharp smack to the side of his thigh made him catch his breath. The resulting warmth wrapped around his groin and straight to his balls.

"You like that, Josh?" He smacked him again, this time on the other thigh. "Are you a bad omega who needs to be reminded who is boss?"

"Yes." Josh jerked his hips, meeting Stone thrust for thrust.

"You going to let me take care of you, baby. This is my ass to please and spank now, right?"

"Yes. Yes." Josh had streaked beyond formulating

anything resembling coherent thoughts. All he wanted was the sparkling orgasm that dangled just out of his reach.

"Stroke yourself. I want to feel your cum on my chest. Mark me, Josh. Make me yours."

Josh followed Stone's instructions and it only took a moment before the sparkles dancing in his peripheral thoughts melted into a massive wave of pleasure. It coursed through him with the power of a hurricane, sweeping them both away.

They lay there panting for a few minutes, wrapped in each other's arms. Josh couldn't stop stroking the sweat-covered muscles wrapped over Stone's shoulders and arms.

Stone untangled Josh's legs from his shoulders and kissed him gently. Josh wrapped his arms around Stone preventing him from getting up. "Let go for a moment, baby. I want to get something to clean us up and then I promise we'll snuggle."

Bone-crushing loneliness hit Josh when Stone crawled out of bed. *What exactly did I just do?* He'd jumped into bed with a man he hardly knew and who was strong enough to tear him limb from limb. *Is this why my mom hooked up with men who beat her? She traded her body for security and ended up in a worse* place. Am I following in her footsteps?

Chapter Five

The next three days went by in a blur. For a tiny little thing, George took up the vast majority of his and Josh's time; constant feedings day and night. Josh's irrational fear something would happen to their kitten exhausted them both. The vet had warned them, all kittens were different in how often they wanted to eat, but it seemed like George's hunger never ended. Three days of warmth, love, and a continuously full tummy did wonders for the little bundle of fur.

When they weren't caring for the furry little piglet, Stone helped Josh set up his yarn shop and organize all the stock he unpacked. They drove into Rapid City and set up a delivery address so he could pick up his supplies and send online orders out in the future. The entire time Josh clenched his hands together and vibrated like a nervous ball of anxiety, which pissed

Stone off. He wanted his mate to feel safe and secure but failed in all of his attempts.

What they shared the first night branded Stone for eternity. He'd noticed a difference in Josh the moment he came out of the bathroom. In retrospect, maybe he should have snuggled first because his mate emotionally retreated, and now Stone felt as if he was back at square one. He wanted to talk to Josh about renting out part of the shop downstairs but didn't want to pressure his mate. The need to hold him and mark him grew exponentially every day but so did the fears his mate wouldn't ever accept him. He'd all but moved into Josh's apartment under the guise of sharing kitten duty but he hoped the close proximity would make it easier to get past the emotional walls Josh hid behind. "I think he eats more than I do," Josh commented while the kitten hogged out on a tiny bottle of formula. "My mom used to say boys had a hollow leg but I think all four of George's are."

Stone sat down on the bed next to Josh. Three in the morning and he'd been in the middle of an incredible dream about fucking his mate silly when George started fussing and woke them both up. Sitting back against the headboard, he rubbed his face and scratched his beard. Despite the exhaustion weighing on his body, his head and cock wanted to reenact every delicious moment of his dream. In his head, he bent Josh over a log in the forest and drove his cock deep into his ass while howling at the large moon hanging over them.

Not being moon bound, he didn't usually pay attention to the lunar cycles, but a glance out the window proved they were only days away from a full one. He took a close look at his mate and noticed something he'd missed in the past couple of days. He could blame the sleep deprivation for not being as tuned-in as he should have been, but it didn't matter. Guilt slammed into him as he noticed the distinct signs of strain around Josh's features. His eyes looked haunted and his movements were stiff and almost uncoordinated. His dreadlocks hung limp around his face, and his shoulder curved like he carried too much weight.

"Josh, are you moon bound?" Stone leaned forward and slid his hand down Josh's bare spine. He slept nude but Josh always wore boxers or sleep pants to bed. A habit Stone hoped to talk him out of one day soon.

"Kind of. I can shift if I'm in danger or really

stressed out, but I'm not strong enough to resist a full moon." His shoulders drooped as if he'd been handed a death sentence. The full moon was usually something to look forward to with moon-bound shifters because it gave them a chance to let their wolves free for a couple of nights.

"Talk to me, baby." He moved closer to his mate, slipping his legs on either side of him. Stone wrapped his arms around Josh's waist and closed the distance between his chest and Josh's back. Looking over Josh's shoulder, he watched George flop over to the side after demolishing his bottle.

Josh sighed, leaning back into his embrace. The small gesture of trust filled him with joy. He gently stroked his hand across Josh's belly while he reached out and gently patted their kitten. "I'm going to crack up it he lets out a massive burp." Josh snickered, exactly the response Stone hoped for.

Sitting in companionable silence, they watched George as he wriggled and played in Josh's lap until he exhausted himself and fell asleep. The little guy had gotten so much stronger and healthy looking in the last couple of days, he didn't look anything like the dying bundle of fur Stone had found by the river.

"I'm scared." The quiet, emotional words ripped at

Stone's heart. *Why doesn't he believe I'll protect him to my last breath?* The words sat on the tip of his tongue, but he held back. If Josh was finally ready to talk, he didn't want to ruin the moment.

"It's been three days and nothing. I don't believe he went away and every second all I can think about is what if he returns. I'm afraid he's going to do something to hurt you or George. I still think I should leave before someone dies."

"Why are they hunting you, Josh?" Stone didn't think Josh simply disappeared into the night without managing to retaliate against his former pack. Why else would they be searching for him? Josh didn't believe in himself but Stone could see the strength in his mate and believed in him.

"I don't know," Josh mumbled as he pulled away to take George to his nest. He shuffled back a minute later, pausing before crawling into bed. Rolling onto his side, he arced away from Stone. "We can talk in the morning."

You are not dismissing me that easily. Stone had gone out of his way to prove to Josh he wouldn't do anything to hurt him, and he refused to let his sweet, stubborn mate get away with avoiding this conversation. A sharp tug rolled Josh under him.

Stone laced their fingers together and pinned his hands to the bed on either side of Josh's head. "Nope, we are talking now. You're holding back information which could get someone killed, you or an innocent. Neither is acceptable in my book."

Stone could hide behind the persona of a pack protector, but there was so much more to this. He'd always thought the Black Hills as home but something had been missing. Now, he understood home wasn't simply a place. Home was the sweet omega beneath him. Wherever he could ensure his mate's safety. *And I can't ensure shit if he doesn't confess to this, whatever it is.*

Josh shook his head and closed his eyes, as if Stone would go away. *Not happening, lover.* He tugged on his hands but Stone kept them anchored where they were. "It's late. We're both tired. I'll tell you in the morning."

"I can't protect you if you don't admit what you did."

Josh's eyes flew open and Stone saw the anger brewing behind them. "What makes you think I did anything?"

Good, get pissed and ready to fight for your freedom. "Because, I don't believe you snuck off with your tail between your legs like a whipped dog. The man tormented you and made your life hell. I bet whatever you took meant a lot to him." He watched Josh's reactions carefully and when his mate's eyes opened almost comically wide, he knew he'd gotten it right. "You hit him where it counted, right in his ego. What did you take?"

"A ring," Josh sighed, his anger deflated. "A goddamn ring he kept in his safe and only brought out on special occasions. He used to brag about being sent to take out a pack encroaching on his lands. According to him, he killed the Alpha himself. Taking that ring was the biggest mistake I've ever made. I should have run away with my tail between my legs. "

"Where is it now?"

"Let me up and I'll get it."

Stone let him go and Josh moved off the bed to crouch on the floor. He returned a minute later with a large silver ring in his palm, a large bear head with what looked like sapphires for eyes.

"Donnovan is smaller than you and, to be honest, I don't know how he did it. Judging by the size of this ring, the alpha had been either huge or had really fat fingers."

Stone held out his hand and Josh dropped the

heavy ring in his palm. He closed his fingers around it before catching Josh with his other hand. "Come here."

Josh came into his arms with a sigh. When he curled up against Stone's chest, something clicked deep inside and the distinct feeling he'd found his place in the universe returned, stronger than ever. "I'm keeping the ring, Josh." Stone opened the drawer in the nightstand, dropped the ring into it, and retrieved the lube. "If he wants it, he's going to have to come to me to get it."

When Josh looked up at him, he slid his hand over the dreadlocks flopped over the worried face. He had the most expressive brown eyes and Stone wanted to demand he acknowledge the mating pull between them. *I never should have made that damn promise. All he wanted was to bind Josh to him. What am I waiting for again?*

"Why would you? You're putting yourself in danger."

"I'm protecting you." He stroked his thumb along Josh's lower lip. "You're more important than anything else."

"Because you're a pack protector?"

"No. I want to tear apart every creature who ever

made you doubt your self-worth." Stone stifled the growling anger building in his chest and covered Josh's mouth with a hand when it looked like he planned to argue. "You are the most important living being in the universe to me. I'll always put you first."

Josh frowned at him over his fingers and licked his palm. "I'll remove my hand only if you promise not to say anything. Just kiss me."

He lifted his hand and Josh lurched up, attacking Stone's mouth. The simmering passion that never quite subsided between them flared to life. An inferno of desire wrapped around them both.

"I never believed...I'd find...." Josh gasped between kisses. Stone didn't give him a chance to finish the sentence. Their tongues danced together as they kissed and he tore Josh's boxers from his body. His mate made a soft, dismayed sound but Stone didn't apologize. From now on, he planned to destroy anything Josh wore to bed until he learned to sleep naked.

They wrestled for position, rolling around on the bed as they explored each other's bodies. Josh was stronger than his slim physique looked, but he couldn't defeat Stone's bulkier muscles. They were both panting with need by the time Stone got him pinned on his belly, his ridged cock resting on the crack of Josh's ass. Stone's hair slid over Josh's back and he moaned, a delicious needy sound that almost had him coating Josh's ass with his cum.

"Would you let me fuck you, Stone?"

"Absolutely, just not right now. I've been thinking about sinking into your ass all day." Stone also had a plan which required Josh stay put. "I won't last long if I'm thinking about you riding my ass." He reached around Josh's hips, to stroke him. "You have a sweet arch. It's going to peg my prostate with every stroke and drive me insane."

Josh didn't speak. Instead he made sweet needy cries as his body quivered under Stone's. For a moment, he almost forgot his plan but managed to pull his cock back at the last moment. He shimmied down Josh's body and parted his ass cheeks. Flicking his tongue out, he rimmed the sweet pucker hidden within. The lush aroma of lust permeated the air as he licked and teased his partner. By the time he got the lube, Stone feared he'd never last.

A few strokes with his lubed-up fingers stretched Josh enough before he pressed the tip of his cock against the entrance to paradise. "Gonna fuck you good, baby."

"Yes, yes do it."

Stone pushed past the initial ring of muscle, taking things slow so he didn't cause any damage but Josh kept rocking his ass back, quickening the pace. Stone had no intention of waiting for his mate to accept him. His wolf rode him hard, trying to make him understand the imperative. Where his human side fixated on promises and repercussions, his wolf focused on basic needs. Josh had been told lie after lie in his life. Only actions would prove how much Stone loved him, and he didn't have any doubt the immense feeling in his chest was love.

Anchoring Josh's body against his, Stone lifted him up as he sat back on his heels with Josh's legs sprawled out over his thighs. The position allowed him more control and he rocked them both, jacking his pelvis back and forth. "Oh yeah. I'm going to make you mine. Okay, baby?"

"Yes! Now! God yes!"

With the affirmative response, Stone sank his teeth into the sensitive spot where Josh's neck met his shoulder. Joy pure and exquisite slammed into him, robbing him of all human thought. His instincts kicked in and he fucked his mate into a screaming orgasm that pulled him right along with him and had them both howling at the ceiling.

***

"Look at me."

The strength in his mate's voice woke Stone, and he opened his eyes to discover Josh leaning over him. Stretching, he rolled over and leaned closer to him, their faces only a few inches apart on the pillow. They'd both collapsed after the most phenomenal orgasm of his life. He knew asking to mate Josh while he was out of his mind with lust was sneaky, but he couldn't summon any sense of guilt. "Yes, baby. What would you like?"

"You claimed me." There wasn't any censorship in Josh's tone, just complete and total shock. Josh's eyes were wide and slightly glazed, confusion swirling in them. He lay there running his fingertips over Stone's mark on his neck.

"Yes, I did."

"Why?"

"Because you're mine and I decided I couldn't wait any longer for you to see it for yourself. By claiming you, my wolf isn't as agitated and pushing at me all the time."

113

"But, it's not complete. I didn't bite you."

"No, you didn't. That's for you to decide, but I'm not going anywhere, Josh, so if it takes you a couple of decades, then I'll have to have patience." I hope. He leaned close and pressed a quick kiss against Josh's swollen, red lips. He looked well and truly ravished and Stone's body started to react again to his mate's scent. Nothing would stop him from responding when his mate was within arm's reach, and he had every intention of keeping him close.

Tomorrow he would fill Drew in on the situation and then put a stop to it. He wouldn't pressure Josh, but he would eliminate the distractions and obstacles between them.

Chapter Six

Josh dropped the skeins back into a box and paced the showroom. Trying to focus on sorting out yarn took too much concentration. Hell, he didn't know if he would be kicked out of town or worse. Would Stone come with me? Josh never contemplated the ramifications in being claimed. The idea of having a soul mate had been an impossible dream. Growing up, he'd been constantly reminded omegas were a burden to a pack. After he reflected on what he knew about Paul and Tasha, he understood what they experienced didn't break them, just like he didn't break. They all carried scars but they were survivors. Maybe I am stronger than I thought.

The squeak of the stairs and heavy footsteps alerted him to Stone's return. He'd been up in the apartment talking to their alpha on the phone, while feeding George, filling him in on Eddie and the ring. His epiphany of strength drained away at the prospective news. Stone opened the door and Josh's heart fell. His eyes were dark and his expression serious.

"You look like we're about to go in front of a firing squad. Hit me with it. Fast."

Stone winced when Josh said hit, rubbing his beard with his open hand. "Drew's pretty sure he knows who your natural father was."

"Oh, that's it?" He'd been expecting devastating news, not confirmation of what he already suspected. Stone's use of the word was left him little doubt. "Did he leave or is he dead?"

"Garrick died in a dominance challenge last year."

"Shit." Josh pulled the bandana off his head and rubbed his dreadlocks, massaging his scalp at the same time. He pulled the fabric through his fingers while sorting out the emotions flowing through him. "I know he wasn't a good man. Why else would my mother have run away from him? I don't know if she ever told him she'd allowed him to get her pregnant. I guess part of me hoped he'd changed and I didn't have tainted DNA."

"Baby, you're not tainted." Stone grabbed his hand

116

and lifted it, brushing his lips across his palm. "You are all the good bits of your entire family tree condensed into one gorgeous, sexy man."

Josh looked up at Stone; if anyone were to see him in a dark alley, they'd probably take off running, but he could be the kindest man who'd ever lived. "You're just blinded by my awesomeness and can't see the truth."

"That's a distinct possibility." Stone winked at him before reaching out to blatantly cup his crotch. "I'm willing to accept you and all your imagined faults."

The blood drained from his body to his groin so fast Josh almost saw stars. "You don't have a shy bone in your body, do you?"

"Nope, why bother? You're my mate and I've claimed you." He wiggled his eyebrows, the seriousness of earlier melting away under the heat of his gaze. "I'm still focused on convincing you I'd be the best mate ever."

"Really? How brave are you?"

"Try me."

That challenge was too good to pass up. "Do you know when Drew is arriving?" Josh reached out and tugged on the silver button of Stone's jeans. The moment it gave, he slipped his hand inside and pressed the zipper down with the back of his hand.

Stone choked on his breath, shaking his head no. "The shop door's unlocked."

Josh dropped to his knees at Stone's feet. "Then our alpha might see more than he expected." He angled the hot, hard cock out from behind the denim. Sliding his fingers over the entire length and enjoying the silky feel, he gently eased the foreskin back. The musky taste of his lover coated his tongue as Josh laved the head of his cock. Stone grabbed handfuls of his hair, lifting it out of the way as Josh wrapped his lips around the blunt head and sucked him into his mouth. He peered up from under his lashes and watched as Stone dropped his head back on his shoulders. The tendons lining his neck stood out, and a low growl echoed in the room.

Such a gorgeous reaction made Josh feel like a god. He needed the distraction from his thoughts and Stone was the perfect target. He loved knowing he could reduce this big man to a quivering mass by doing something so simple and enjoyable. Slurping and tonguing Stone's length, he treating the thick erection like a melting ice cream cone. The skin felt hot under his tongue, deceptively silky and smooth and hard as marble.

"Oh, fuck you have a hot little mouth."

Stone's hips jerked and he mumbled an apology when he pushed deeper than Josh had been expecting. Knowing Stone's control frayed, he leaned forward, sucking the thick rod over his tongue, relaxing his throat, taking him as deep as possible. He pulled back, swirling his tongue around his length, licking the slightly salty pre-cum welling up at the tip.

"Yes, that's it, fuck again. God, do it again," Stone rambled on. His eyes were bright, glowing amber as his wolf surged to the surface.

Feeling empowered Josh deep throated him again, keeping eye contact with him as he did. Stone snarled, his lips curling up, baring his teeth. Aggressive arousal had a scent all its own and didn't scare Josh in the least. He took Stone's length over and over as he gripped his thickly muscled thighs. For the first time in his life, Josh's wolf pushed forward, Stone's delectable scent drawing him out from hiding.

His eyes must have changed because Stone bent over as best he could; gripping Josh's hair he stared down into his face. "There you are, you sweet thing. Stay with me, Josh. Take every drop I give you."

Josh growled low in his throat, feeling the vibrations reverberate along Stone's cock. His mate tilted his head upward and let loose a howl before he bathed Josh's tongue with his salty essence. Josh's cock pulsed in warning, the sensitivity so acute that even the most simple of touches would set him off.

Stone scooped Josh up and dropped him onto the counter, pulling down his pants, and engulfed Josh's cock between heartbeats. One good long suck pushed him over his limit. Josh gripped Stone's shoulders and screamed out his name as he emptied his balls down his throat.

"Holy shit, I've never come so fast in my life." Josh's heart hammered double time as he gasped for breath. Stone rose up and kissed him deep; their lips melded together and the rest of the world melted away. "Thank you," he breathed against Stone's lips.

"Don't thank me, it was my pleasure. You're amazing, baby."

A sharp knock at the door reminded Josh they were expecting Drew. "Crap." He struggled with his pants, somehow managing to get his legs tangled in them as he panicked.

"At least he didn't walk straight in." Stone chuckled as he tucked himself back in and then helped Josh get sorted out.

Josh's body morphed from the hot flush of sexual completion to cold fear in the matter of heartbeats. He hadn't expected Drew to arrive this quickly or he never would have started anything. Stone went over to open the shop door and Josh straightened the buttons on his shirt.

Physically, Drew didn't have Stone's bulk, but the energy he radiated made him feel larger than life. It was something only alphas could manage and Josh only dreamed of. He'd spent most of his life hating being an omega. While he lived amongst the humans, he almost felt normal. Being surrounded by a pack again only reinforced his weakness compared to everyone else.

Ryker, the pack enforcer, entered behind Drew. Where the alpha radiated authority, Ryker emanated power and judgment. Neither of them scented the air, but the smirk Drew wore proved he knew exactly what they'd been up to.

"Alpha. Sir." He nodded at both men and stuck his hands in his pockets to hide how hard they were shaking. "How are you both today?"

"Everything is good," Drew said. He looked around at the stock Josh had unpacked and placed on the shelves. "You have a lot more string than I expected. It looks good in here. I hope you do well."

Stone came up next to him and wrapped his arm around his shoulders. Feeling his big strong body next to his went a long way toward shoring up his courage.

"I see you're taking your position as pack protector seriously."

"Josh is mine. I pledge to always protect the pack as long as you're alpha, but Josh will always come first."

"Fair enough." Drew nodded. "Josh, Stone told me about this Eddie and some of the history with your old pack. I need to know where your loyalties are. If you still feel any ties to your old pack, then I need to know now."

Josh shook his head. "No, nothing. I'm loyal to you and the Black Hills Pack. I'm so sorry they followed me here. I'd hoped they wouldn't ever find me."

"Pack gossip travels fast," Drew replied. "They were bound to find out sooner or later you'd come home."

Ryker grunted from his position at the door, and Drew looked over his shoulder at him and nodded as if they were having a silent conversation. "What's done is done. Now, where is this ring Stone told me about?"

"I have it." Stone reached into his pocket and passed the large silver ring over to Drew.

He held it up and looked at it from all angles before passing it back to Ryker. "What do you think?"

Ryker glanced down at it before passing it back. "I was right."

Josh didn't know what any of them were talking about, but neither man seemed overly concerned. That went a long way toward reassuring him. "I can stay?"

Drew turned a surprised look at him. "Of course you can. Don't worry about this." He held up the ring. "I have some suspicions about it, but we'll take care of it."

Ryker opened the shop door and nodded at them before stepping out. Drew followed, pausing in the doorway to turn. "Both of you be careful and let me know if this Eddie shows up. Don't kill him before I have a chance to ask him some questions."

"No promises," Stone answered. Drew seemed satisfied with his response and left with a wave.

Josh took a deep breath, feeling like a deflated

balloon as he sagged against Stone's strength. "Do you think they mean it?"

"Yes, baby. Drew Tao doesn't say anything he doesn't mean. This is your home now and you're a part of his pack. You even have your own personal protector at your beck and call."

A small kernel of hope flickered in his heart. He reached up and ran his fingers over his shoulder, rubbing the spot where Stone marked him. Physically, it had healed, but the area tingled every time Stone touched him. "You mentioned before about wanting to share this space with me. There's more than enough room."

"I'd like that very much, but let's worry about one thing at a time. How are we going to draw Eddie out?"

The last thing Josh wanted to think about was Eddie, but he knew he couldn't look toward his future without dealing with his past first.

***

Stone couldn't be prouder of his mate. Josh carried an incredible core of steel within him and he didn't understand how Josh could think of himself as weak. He hated the haunted look behind those gorgeous eyes and much preferred the memory of his mate's eyes when they were filled with passion. A golden ring circled Josh's brown irises, giving them an ethereal look when Stone sucked his cock and he wanted to see it again...soon.

The forests would be alive tonight with reveling moon-bound shifters. That kind of pandemonium could hide a great number of tragedies. If Eddie chose tonight to hunt Josh, it would be the bastard's last mistake. Eddie didn't know the entire pack would be hunting tonight. Stone needed to be sure of Josh's safety and elected to stay with him. What good would his skills be if he left him unprotected to hunt the fucker down and Josh got hurt.

When the moon rose high and bright, Stone felt the soft tugging of it calling to his wolf but he didn't need to answer. Josh shifted the moment the clouds parted and the moonlight shone down on them. He scanned the area. As Josh darted around the yard, he looked longingly at the forest line across the street and then back at Stone. "Don't even think of it. Not tonight, until we know for sure the asshole has left the area."

Eddie might have gone back to his pack to report,

but Stone believed the slimy bastard arrogant enough to think he could bring Josh back on his own.

He crouched in the grass and Josh raced over to him, pressing his body against Stone's thigh. "We should really go back inside but I know it sucks to be a wolf indoors."

He scratched the tawny wolf behind the ears. "You're so beautiful." His sweet mate stretched out next to his legs and flopped on his back for a tummy rub. Stone was happy to give him what he wanted, and if it meant crouching here coddling his mate he'd happily do it. "And greedy. I bet you'd lie here all night and let me do this." Josh let his tongue flop out of his mouth and panted, his tail waving back and forth against the grass.

The chilly breeze shifted and Stone caught the faint scent of gun oil on it. His wolf howled and his muscles bunched before he grabbed Josh. His senses tuned in to the threat, and he heard a distinct click a split second before the ground exploded where Josh had been lying. What kind of pathetic asshole used a gun? It had to be Eddie. The idiot probably figured everyone would blame it on hunters or something equally stupid.

Stone kept rolling with his mate in his arms,

building the momentum to fling the wolf into the back of his pickup. "Stay down!" he shouted, leaping to his feet. A shot ricocheted off the back of his truck, the low ting noise echoed in the night air. He ducked and leapt to the side. *If I can draw his fire away....* "Try to shift back. There's clothes next to you. Get in the cab and drive!"

Stone shifted, leaping in random unpredictable directions as he inched closer to the tree line. He'd figured out what direction the shots were coming from and planned to kill the motherfucker as soon as he got within range. A low howl ripped through the air, followed by another, and Stone felt a glimmer of hope. Their pack had heard the shots and were headed this way. He paused behind a tree, tilted his head back, and howled, putting all his fury into the sound. He looked toward the forest and then back to the truck, torn between eviscerating the bastard shooting at his mate or staying and assuring Josh's safety.

It only took a moment to decide before Stone turned and ran back toward the truck. He heard a couple more shots go off but they weren't aimed at him. More howls echoed under the moon, letting him know that the pack hunted down the intruder.

Concern for his mate overrode his sense of self-preservation. Ensuring Josh's safety was his primary concern right now.

He raced back to the truck and found Josh curled up in a ball in the corner. He'd managed to shift back into human form and pulled on the clothes left for him. "Baby, you okay?"

Josh looked up, his face drained of color, and he shook like a leaf in the wind. Stone crawled into the truck bed and curled around his body. "It's okay. I won't let anyone hurt you, ever again."

"Don't you ever try to take a bullet for me again." Josh surprised him by thumping him hard on the chest with his fist. "I lay here feeling sick and useless listening to the gun going off not knowing if you were okay."

Stone didn't bother responding because no matter what he said it would be a lie. He'd always stand between a threat and his mate. "Let's get inside where it's safer. We can check on George, too."

The howls from the pack echoed in the distance, and Stone carefully scented the air before allowing Josh to lift his head. When he was certain they were safe, he grabbed Josh's hand and they raced for the shop's back door. Once inside Stone breathed a sigh of relief and hugged Josh. "It'll be okay."

Josh raced upstairs and Stone followed him. After checking on George who slept on his back with his arms and legs sprawled out like a starfish, Josh eagerly returned to Stone's arms.

"What if they come back and endanger the pack and the town? I still think I should go."

"Wherever you go, I go." Stone pulled Josh closer and wrapped his arms around him. The sound of a gunshot hitting the ground where his mate lay a split second before would haunt him for the rest of his life. He'd finally found the one person in the universe made just for him and almost lost him. Nuzzling Josh's neck below his ear, he flicked his tongue out along the mark he'd given him. "You're my home, Josh. Right here. This is my place. I hope you like having me around because it's going to be a long time before I let you out of my sight."

Josh leaned back and looked down at him. His eyes sparkled with moisture and Stone could see the love in his heart reflected back at him. "For the first time in my life, I feel safe, Stone. It has nothing to do with the Black Hills or with the pack and everything to do with having your arms around me."

"I love you, Josh. If you want me to carry you

around for the rest of your life and keep you safe, I'll do it."

"I love you, too, Stone, but I'd hate to accidentally stab you with a knitting needle." Josh traced his fingers down the side of Stone's cheek, his whiskers caressing the pads of his fingers. "I want to claim you, too."

"There's nothing else in the universe I want more. Claim me, because you're the keeper of my heart now. I want to know I'll always have a home with you."

"I love you." Josh brushed his lips against Stone's. The light teasing touch was enough to send shivers along his limbs, raising his body's awareness. The little minx pushed against his shoulders and he willingly dropped back against their bed, stretching his legs out. After Josh unwrapped the soft scarf from around his neck, Stone plucked it from his fingers and brought it to his nose. It didn't smell simply of prey but of his prey. "I want to wear these so I have your scent right next to me every moment of the day."

Josh launched himself at Stone and tore at his clothes. "I want you, right now." It appeared he wasn't the only one feeling some post-violence arousal. Nothing better than fucking after fighting.

"Here. I don't mind a bit of a burn, fuck I just want to feel you inside me." Josh had a small packet of lube in the back pocket of his jeans and passed it to him.

"Whatever my sweet mate wants." Stone tore the packet open and made good use of it getting Josh ready.

"I want you. Only you."

"You and me, baby."

Assured Josh could handle it, he plunged in. Snapping his hips back and forth, he slammed his cock into Josh, reveling in the gasps and ecstasy-filled cries spilling from his sweet lips. "That's right, baby. You like the feel of my cock, don't you?"

"Yes!"

"You going to stay with me forever, be mine, let me fuck you whenever I want?"

"Yes!" Josh gasped for air and squeezed Stone's arms so tightly he could feel his nails piercing the skin on his inner arms.

"Are you mine, Josh?"

"Yes!"

"Do you love me?" Stone pushed into Josh's body and froze, watching the expression on his face as the question sank into his head. The words hung in the air and Josh blinked up at him, a moment of clarity, and Stone watched as Josh thought about lying. His little mate couldn't lie to save his life. The truth blazed all over his face.

"Yes," he whispered.

"Good." Desire slammed into him, a bundle of love for the man beneath him echoing around his thoughts, making his wolf howl, or maybe he howled? Moments before he knew his balls were going to erupt, he pressed his face into the crook of Josh's neck, slamming his cock into Josh's ass. He continued to peg his mate's sweet spot, prolonging his orgasm until Stone allowed his own release to wash over him. His face in Josh's neck, inhaling his scent, he reamed his ass, blowing his load deep into his mate.

Before his orgasmic bliss could abate, Josh snarled out a single word. "Mine." He grabbed Stone's head and pushed it to the side. His teeth sank into Stone's shoulder, and, in that moment, an emotional tie snapped into place between them. Josh's joy rushed through Stone and back, creating a vortex of pleasure that had his cock erupting a second time. Josh's seed spilled out warm on his stomach, and an incredible peace stretched out over his thoughts.

"Forever," he whispered against Josh's hair.

Chapter Seven

Josh leaned back against Stone's chest; the warmth seeped past his T-shirt. He loved how warm his mate always felt. Stone had gotten a text from Drew a few minutes earlier to meet Ryker outside. They were sitting on the tail of Stone's truck when Ryker came out of the forest. They were going to go in and check on George when the enforcer appeared. Josh's nerves kicked into high gear. Please let this be over.

"You both okay?" he asked as they met in the middle of the road.

"Yes, how's everyone else?" Stone asked. "Did you catch the gunman?"

"Shooter's name was Eddie." Ryker crossed his arms over his chest. "He's got the ring and will be sent back to his pack."

"What if he comes back to get me or doesn't give it

to Donnovan?" Josh couldn't believe it could be this easy. Why didn't he just kill him? "The man is a pathological liar." His brain raced with the possible problems in leaving him alive. Josh wasn't completely bloodthirsty but feared someone could get hurt because of him.

Ryker's expression darkened as if he didn't want to answer any more questions. Two weeks ago, the dark look would have sent Josh to his knees. But, now, secure in the knowledge Stone wouldn't allow anyone to hurt him, he didn't back down. Although, he did lower his eyes. He didn't want Ryker to think he issued a challenge.

"Drew and I decided to send the ring back in Eddie's mouth." Ryker scowled, obviously unimpressed he needed to explain. From the look on his face and sharp angle to his jaw, Josh knew he wouldn't get any more information.

"I don't get it." Josh couldn't see why the man would carry the ring in his mouth or why it would stop his stepfather from retaliating. Panic clawed at him. Don't they realize this will never be over? Eddie would come back because Donnovan would order him to and they would be in the same position as they were the other day. Only, now, they wouldn't know when to expect an attack.

"Shhh," Stone whispered against his temple, skimming his back in long, soothing strokes. "I think what Ryker is trying to say is they're sending the asshole's head back with the ring in his mouth."

Any other time, Josh would have gagged at the mental image Stone's explanation created, but not this time. Relief filled him at the knowledge he wouldn't have to look over his shoulder anymore. Essentially, his violent stepfather was a bully, and Josh felt confident the old man wouldn't risk retaliation by continuing to threaten Josh.

"We've made it clear to Donnovan. If he tries anything against our pack, we'll take him apart." With a sharp nod, Ryker melted back into the shadows of the trees, leaving them alone.

"Damn."

"What is it?" Stone wrapped his arms around Josh's waist and pressed an openmouthed kiss against his neck.

"If I'd known he planned to send back Eddie's head, I might have knitted a hat to keep his ears warm."

"That's sick." Stone growled and licked the shell of his ear. "There might be hope for you yet."

Josh angled his head to allow his mate more access, his cock twitching with excitement. Between heartbeats, the concern weighing on his shoulders lifted away. Wolf justice was swift and brutal but effective. To prevent the potential for attacks against their pack, Josh understood why Drew sent the ring back with the enforcer's head. *I wish I could see Donnovan's face when it arrives.*

"I love the taste of your skin." Stone nipped the muscle at the base of Josh's neck, licking the skin where he'd left his mating mark. The caress sent waves of shivers along his spine.

Josh lifted his arms and wrapped them back around Stone's head. "You can taste me any time you want but I know some places that taste better than my neck."

"Do you now." Stone spun him around so they were face-to-face.

Josh looked up at the beautiful smile on Stone's face. The fear which iced his veins in the past melted away, allowing the heat behind the promise in his smile to warm Josh's insides. "How did I get so lucky?"

"Because you needed me as much as I needed you."

"I don't know how you see that."

"And I don't know how you can't. We were both craving a family and love. But we had to come home to find it."

"I wish I was a stronger mate for you."

"I told you before, you underestimate yourself, Josh. You are strong. You were brave enough to come here and start a new life. You took a chance on everyone including me when you had no reason to believe anyone would treat you differently than you'd experienced. I insisted on running these hills for weeks while I decided if I could take a chance. If it hadn't been for you, I might still be running."

"Nice try, but you already decided to stay before you met me."

"No, I decided to stay when all I could smell was prey and I wanted to hunt. My wolf knew something special waited for me here. It took me a bit longer to figure it out."

He rose on tiptoe and teased Stone with a playful kiss. "I'm glad your wolf is smarter than you."

Stone anchored their bodies together, "So am I, beautiful. This is forever. Now, about my sweater...."

"If I knit you something out of alpaca, you're still going to smell like prey, you know."

"No, I'll smell like you."

Josh's heart skipped a beat. I could never love this man any more than I already do. "What color do you want?"

"You pick." Stone nuzzled his nose against his neck sending a wave of delicious shivers down his limbs. His hand stroked a path down Josh's spine, feeling equally as possessive as reassuring.

"I was thinking about the shop and what to call it." Josh wanted Stone to understand he believed they were partners in everything, not just their souls. "What do you think of String 'n Ink?"

The rhythmic stroking ceased and Stone looked down at him. His eyes shone bright and full of love. "You mean it? Combining our businesses? Do you think it will work?"

"I think we're the first combination yarn shop and tattoo studio in the world, but we already have a shop mascot in George as soon as he gets big enough to make it down the stairs. It's our home and business all in one."

Stone's mouth opened and shut a couple of times before he gave up speaking. Instead he bent down and gave Josh the most passionate kiss of his life. Josh put every ounce of love he felt for the big man into the kiss and got back more in return. When the kiss ended, the two of them stood there staring at each other. Josh would bet his grin looked as goofy as the one on Stone's face.

"Did I tell you about my dream, baby?"

Josh shook his head, not sure what point Stone wanted to make.

"It involved you bent over a fallen tree during a full moon."

"I'm a wolf during a full moon, you weirdo." Over time, Josh had learned the fun in teasing his mate. It was a freedom he'd never known before, teasing someone and not fearing a violent retaliation. "Bestiality is nasty and you say I'm sick."

Stone swatted his ass. His jeans dulled the smack, but Josh loved the playful impact. His enjoyment must have shone on his face because Stone's gaze narrowed and his eyes shone with mischief. "Like that, huh? Good to know. Maybe we should find a tree to bend you over and I'll spank your ass until you beg me to fuck it."

"You'll have to catch me first." Josh dug his fingers against the muscles wrapped around Stone's hips. As he'd hoped, Stone yelped and jumped back, allowing Josh to take off.

"Tickle me, will you? You're going to get it now!" Stone's deep voice boomed through the trees as Josh ran. Joy rushed through him and bubbled up in his laughter. The delighted sound bounced off the large trees around him. Unlike the last time Stone chased him through these trees, he couldn't wait to be caught.

About the Author

Best selling author Kayleigh Malcom (and her alter ego Corinne Davies) is a firm believer that all love is beautiful and everyone deserves a Happily Ever After....well, except for those involved with cancelling Firefly. She's still holding a grudge over that one.

She first put pen to paper in an attempt to write a love story between her and her favourite rock singer of the time. It was filled with all the angst that only a teenager can come up with and, of course, an incredible wardrobe. Years later, during the wee hours of the morning, when her first daughter insisted on waking up, she discovered online RPGs and her love of writing emerged again.After many encouraging words from fellow writers, she decided to try her hand at developing her own stories, learning it takes more than mind blowing sex and a happily ever after to make a great story.

By day, she is a full-time wife, mother, and product consultant. At night, she avoids such mundane tasks as housework and laundry by creating her own worlds where fantasy and mythology comes to life. Worlds in which you are just as likely to be living next door to an ancient Deity as finding your soul mate in steam powered flying machine. Sticking with one genre is a talent she hasn't achieved yet and can be found creating worlds as normal as our own or as fantastic as her dreams. Her characters have to face real life challenges, as many of us do, but love always finds a way to conquer all.

A social media junkie, she can be found haunting many different sites and loves to hear from her readers.

Also by Kayleigh Malcolm

Claiming His Cub

Pursuing Their Fantasies

Rolling in Sin